PO
OM

W9-AGT-354

WILD WAYMIRE

Other Five Star Titles
by Lewis B. Patten:

Tincup in the Storm Country
Trail to Vicksburg
Death Rides the Denver Stage
The Woman at Ox-Yoke
Ride the Red Trail
Blood on the Grass
Guns of Vengeance
Back Trail
Sundown

WILD WAYMIRE
A Western Duo

Lewis B. Patten

Five Star • Waterville, Maine

First Edition
First Printing: September 2006.

Published in 2006 in conjunction with
Golden West Literary Agency.

Set in 11 pt. Plantin.

Printed in the United States on permanent paper.

Library of Congress Cataloging-in-Publication Data

Patten, Lewis B.
    [They called him a killer]
    Wild Waymire : a western duo / by Lewis B. Patten.
—1st ed.
       p. cm.
    ISBN 1-59414-391-9 (hc : alk. paper)
    1. Western stories. I. Patten, Lewis B. Wild Waymire.
II. Title.
PS3566.A79T47 2006
  813′.54—dc22   2006013251

WILD WAYMIRE

Table of Contents

They Called Him a Killer

I

Sundown was a relief after the blistering day. With but a couple of miles yet to go, Stuart Cannon dismounted at a narrow stream and flung himself flat on the ground to drink from its tepid, alkali water. The flat stones of the creekbed were hot, as though a fire burned beneath them, and Cannon got up quickly with a surprised, low-voiced curse. He rubbed the scorched palms of his hands against the legs of his dusty pants.

Downstream, the horse sucked noisily, greedily, his hide caked with sweat and dust. In the west, the sun turned the sky to copper.

For a moment, Cannon was still, relaxed, and motionless. Then he turned, unbuckled his saddle cinch, and lifted the saddle off to cool the horse's sweaty back. The horse shook itself.

An almost negligible breeze stirred and Cannon faced into it gratefully, fishing without thought in his stained, damp shirt pocket for sack tobacco and papers. He squatted comfortably while he rolled his smoke and touched a match to its end.

A youngish man in his early twenties, he was neither tall nor overly broad. Slight, you would say, until you noticed the breadth of his shoulders and the ripple of muscles under his tight shirt.

His face bore several small hairline cuts, for he had dry-shaved this morning in anticipation of his arrival. It was smooth-skinned, a dark-bronzed face that a careful lack of expression made notable. The eyes were dark, almost black.

11

The brows were also dark, unusually bushy, and made an almost unbroken line across the bridge of his nose, which was straight and somewhat narrow.

This was the face of a man alone, neither accepted by nor accepting society—a man who knew conflict and struggle and rejection, and who had withdrawn into himself as a defense. There was an oddly brooding look to his face, a dark wariness about his eyes. His cheeks were hollow, his cheek bones high. Strong-jawed, firm-lipped, you could imagine neither laughter nor softness ever changing that rigid mold of countenance. Strangely enough, it was this very quality about him that most attracted women. Perhaps his coldness simply presented a challenge. Or perhaps they sensed the warmth so carefully guarded beneath it.

In dress, he conformed to a conventional pattern— down-at-the-heel boots, cracked with age and use, dusty, faded waist overalls, blue shirt, now darkened at armpits, back and chest with sweat, and narrow-brimmed hat, its crown round and uncreased. An aged gun rode low at his right side in an age-hardened holster, but the loops in his cartridge belt were empty of cartridges.

Things pegged a man. Those empty loops pegged Stuart Cannon as a man who carried a gun more from habit and compliance with custom than from any real need. They shouted plainly that he expected the loads in the gun itself to be sufficient for any trouble he was likely to encounter.

Hard, he looked—hard and possessed of a vast competence. So strongly, in fact, did he emanate confidence that the gun didn't seem necessary. You'd look at him twice, wherever you saw him, but he would not draw you with liking as some men do. Rather he would stir in you the vaguest kind of uneasiness. If you analyzed it, as few ever did, you would be reminded of a cat, tolerating human society only because tolerance served its purpose, but never really liking it. This was Stuart Cannon, and he was only what circumstances had made him.

Now he turned his head and stared in the direction he had been traveling, his face sour with distaste.

There it stood, its bleak gray walls rising like an obscene monument out of the desert floor. Gray walls, topped with steel spikes and broken glass. Gray walls, whose tiny windows were barred with steel.

Anger flared briefly in Cannon's eyes, and impatience as well. But he waited until he had finished the cigarette before he stirred. Then he rose and flung the stinking, soggy saddle blanket onto the horse's back. He followed it with the saddle, which he cinched rather loosely. Then he swung himself up and moved out again in the direction of the prison.

There would be, he knew, a town at the prison's base, a town with narrow, littered streets that were more like alleys than anything else. The houses would be squat, flat-roofed adobes, housing an abundance of dirty, dark-skinned children. There would be the inevitable strings of bright peppers hanging from projecting beams, and at this time of day the still air would be filled with the sharp aroma of spicy cooking and cedar wood smoke. Dogs would pick Cannon up by his strange smell at the edge of town and would follow him, yapping savagely, wherever he went.

The largest building in town would probably be the mission of San Marcos. No doubt it would stand facing the plaza, or village square. After his interview with Father Gonzales, Stuart Cannon would find a *cantina* where he'd eat a supper of food that burned him from the tip of his tongue clear to the bottom of his stomach.

He liked none of it, this baked, blistering country, its

food, its people, the errand that brought him here. Then why had he come? Even now, Cannon did not thoroughly understand the why himself. It began, he thought, with a man escaping from prison. No. It began a lot further back than that. Perhaps in reality, the escape was the end—or the beginning of the end.

Still frowning at his own thoughts, Cannon reached the outskirts of the town, which differed in no respect from what he had expected. Three skinny, mangy dogs picked him up and followed, yapping and snapping at his horse's heels. Cannon cursed them silently in his mind.

All roads led to the plaza, and Cannon reached it as gray dusk filtered down through the hot, still air to settle on it. He cut across the treeless, dusty square, threading his way between two ancient brass cannon, now green-black with corrosion. The dogs quit him on the far side in favor of another dog that they approached in their stiff-legged way, hair bristling, teeth bared. The other dog quivered and his tail whipped between his legs, and then the three were on him, snarling and biting until he gained his feet and fled with the three in full cry after him.

Watching, Cannon's face showed a certain cynical bitterness, for he had seen this pattern often repeated in human society.

An idler plucked a plaintive melody from the strings of a guitar, seeming not to notice Cannon but studying him closely all the same. Somewhere, in the distance, a woman screamed imprecations at a silent faceless husband. A child squalled; somewhere closer a jackass brayed.

Cannon dismounted before the mission, a large, adobe building with the usual twin square towers topped with bell cupolas. Between the towers, a cross was silhouetted against the darkening sky.

With his eyes rather bleak, Cannon took time to roll another cigarette and smoke it thoughtfully. His eyes touched the idler, paused, and passed on. Finally he tossed the cigarette away, frowned, and went up the walk toward the mission door.

He removed his hat and ran a hand through his sweat-plastered hair, showing the first uncertainty apparent in him today. Then, with obvious irritation at this, he pushed open the door and went inside.

It was cool here, cool because of the three-foot thick adobe walls, because of the high, vaulted ceiling. Down at the altar, a black-robed woman was kneeling, praying. Cannon stared at her briefly before his eyes began their nervous wandering.

It was, he realized, the first time he had been in a church since boyhood. His expression hardened. *Damn it, that was over.* It had been hard to forget, hard to stop hating so bitterly. But he'd managed it. And now it was all going to be dug up again, a dead thing, long buried, its ugliness exposed to the light of day.

Candles flickered from the altar, furnishing the only light until a black-robed priest came in carrying a lighted taper. The priest saw him, changed direction, and approached. The priest murmured—*"Espere un momento, señor."*—caught himself and said softly in English: "A moment, my son." He continued then, lighting candles in their wall brackets, returning at last to the uncomfortable Stuart Cannon.

Cannon's voice was flat, sounding unnaturally loud and clear: "I'd like to see Father Gonzales."

The priest smiled. "I am Father Gonzales. And you are Stuart Cannon. Am I correct?"

Cannon nodded. He supposed there was some resemblance between himself and his father, which would account for the priest's recognition.

Father Gonzales was a small, graying, gentle man a head shorter than Cannon. His face, dark as antique leather, was seamed with deep creases, giving him an almost gnomish look. He led the way through a door and into a small, austerely furnished room with bare walls of naked adobe.

It was the coolest place Cannon had been in all day. Under the influence of the cool, and of the priest's quiet manner, Cannon felt some of his irritability fading.

The priest said: "You look tired. Some wine, perhaps?"

"Water would be better . . . if it's cool."

From a tall *olla* jar, the priest took a dipperful of water. The jar was made of some kind of porous clay that allowed the contents to seep through and evaporate on the outside. Cannon was pleasantly surprised at the water's coolness. He handed the dipper back, refusing a second drink with a spare shake of his head, and came directly to the point. "Your letter said that he'd escaped. Have they caught him yet?"

Father Gonzales shook his head. His glance was searching, probing, as though Cannon were a printed page that he wished to read and understand.

Cannon's next question was a trifle irritable: "Well, what do you want of me? The law can handle this well enough. The law can catch him and bring him back. Why did you have to bring me into it?"

The priest smiled. "Why did you come into it, my son?"

Anger stirred in Cannon's eyes. "Why? Because you asked me to, that's why. I ought to have had better sense."

"That is not what I meant. I meant to ask why you came. You could have refused. You could have closed your mind to your father's trouble and I would not have blamed you if you had."

Cannon had been wondering the same thing himself for the past five or six days. He said honestly: "I'm not sure. Maybe I came because he's the last blood relation I've got. I've got no use for him, but. . . ." It was obvious that Cannon liked his thoughts to be straight and uncomplicated. Self-doubt was foreign to him and he didn't like it. He growled: "Exactly what do you want from me? You think I can catch him when the law can't?"

The priest's face showed considerable understanding. He murmured: "It was not catching him that I had in mind. It is inevitable that your father will be caught . . . or killed. It was only to prevent his being killed that I sent for you."

Cannon asked rather brutally: "Why should I care whether he's killed or not? You're forgetting what he did to me, what he did to my mother. It took me a long time to stop hating him. Now you want to stir it all up again."

The priest's tone had a forced quietness. "Yet you do care . . . else you would not have come. You are, after all, his son."

Cannon laughed harshly. "Don't hold that against me. I had nothin' to do with it." His anger was rising, anger directed more at himself than at the gentle priest. He said: "Your concern for his life is misplaced. He should have been hung years ago. He's an escaped murderer. He killed my mother in a drunken rage, and worst of all he didn't even remember doing it."

"That is what the jury decided."

II

Cannon didn't even seem to hear. His eyes were brooding, blank. Softly, almost as though he were thinking aloud, he said: "I was twelve when it happened. I had a home, a mother, a father. I went to school and I was just like anyone else. Then one morning I woke up and I had nothing. My mother was dead. My father was in jail for killing her." He shuddered involuntarily with the vividness of this memory. "I came into the kitchen just like I always did. The sun was shining in through the curtains. I heard people talking, and I came into the kitchen and saw her lying on the kitchen floor. Nobody'd moved her or covered her. There was blood all over her. Her hair was matted with it. It was splattered all over the floor. Beside her was a whiskey bottle that had been used to beat her to death." Cannon's face was pale. "They said they found my father passed out not far from where she lay." He looked at the priest dazedly. "Hate's a thin word for what I felt toward him. Hate kept me going for a good many years afterward. It was all I had. After the funeral, nobody seemed to know what to do with me. They said I'd turn out just like him and no one wanted to take me in. But you can't leave a twelve-year-old to shift for himself, can you? So they talked the stableman into taking me. He wanted a free hired hand in the stable, anyway. He took me out of school and I curried horses and forked hay and cleaned stalls from daylight to dark seven days a week. If he'd catch me sleeping, he'd wake me with a strap. So I ran away. There's more, but it all sounds the same. When I was eighteen, I only weighed a hundred and ten pounds. I'd been kicked out of more towns and boarded in more jails. . . ." He snorted disgustedly. "Not because of anything I did, either. But because I was broke, and dirty, and hungry."

He stopped, breathing hard, mildly surprised at the way he had uncorked the years of bitterness.

The priest's voice was soft. "That is all past."

"Sure. I know it's past. I stopped hating him a long time ago. But don't tell me I owe him anything just because I happen to be his son."

The priest sighed. He said patiently: "Do you know where your father has gone?"

Impatiently Cannon said: "How should I know where he's gone?"

"He has gone back to Red Butte."

The significance of that failed to register on Cannon's consciousness. He said: "If you know where he's gone, it ought to be simple enough to catch him. Was he fool enough to tell you where he was going?"

Father Gonzales shook his head. "He said nothing. But I know. Does it mean nothing to you that he should have gone to Red Butte?"

"It means he was a damn' fool," Cannon growled.

Father Gonzales ignored the profanity. "No. It means that he knew he had not killed your mother. It means that he returned to Red Butte to try and find out who did."

Cannon mocked with impatient disgust: "Now I've heard everything. He spends more than ten years in prison not knowing what happened that night because he was too drunk to know. And then suddenly he decides he's innocent. What gave him that idea?"

The priest looked somewhat abashed. "Perhaps I had something to do with it." He went on hurriedly before Cannon could interrupt. "I grew to know your father very well during the years he was here. He confided in me. I learned, among other things, that your father and mother very rarely quarreled. If that were true, there would have been no motive for his killing her, for only during a violent quarrel could he have done what they say he did."

Cannon shook his head. "It won't jell, and you know it won't. My mother had no enemies. She was universally liked and respected in Red Butte. She helped them have their babies and nursed them when they were sick. She belonged to the church. You can cross out robbery as a motive because we were poor and everyone knew it. And women aren't murdered without a mighty powerful reason."

"That is true. But I'm not convinced. I've been at this prison for many years, my son. I have known thousands of convicts during that time . . . the weak . . . the vicious . . . the bitter . . . the insane. I have known others who were gentle and kind. Judging men becomes a kind of instinct after a while. A man knows those who can kill and those who cannot."

Cannon murmured resignedly: "I don't doubt your sincerity. But you're wrong." He was cold, as though by coldness alone he could turn aside the priest's persuasiveness. "How did you find me, by the way?"

The priest brightened. "Another argument that there must be something good in your father. His friends. There are two of them who have stuck by him all these years, coming to see him, writing him. It was through one of these that he learned your whereabouts."

Cannon stirred restlessly.

Father Gonzales began to talk hurriedly, anxiously. "Your father knew you hated him. He thinks you still hate him. He had learned to live in prison, had learned to bear its unbearable monotony. But he never learned to bear the thought of his only son hating him. Why do you suppose he risked his life to escape? Because he wanted to be free? Because he wanted to clear his name?" The priest shook his head. "Not for any of these things, but for something quite different. He wanted to regain the respect of his son. He wanted to make you stop hating him."

Cannon was silent, his face somber.

Obviously encouraged, the priest went on: "He will not let himself be captured, Mister Cannon. He will not allow himself to fail at this last task he has set for himself. He will fight like a wolf if they catch up with him. And then he will truly be a murderer. As for learning anything. . . ." He shrugged. "The sheriff in Red Butte has been notified to watch for him. A man has been dispatched from the prison to Red Butte to assist the sheriff. A third man will follow you when you leave here tonight."

Cannon muttered resignedly: "Just what is it you want me to do?" He had no enthusiasm for this, and his manner plainly showed it. It also showed a certain fatalism, as though he had known all along that in answering the priest's summons he was committing himself to do whatever it was the priest wanted him to do.

"Go to Red Butte. Find your father before the law finds him. Persuade him to give himself up and take upon yourself the task he has set for himself."

"How can I, when I don't believe in it?"

Father Gonzales smiled confidently. "Go to Red Butte and at least find your father and talk to him. In the meantime, try to remember what your father was like before the tragedy. If he was good to you, remember that. Try to give him the benefit of the doubt, to forget what he is supposed to have done."

Cannon grinned sourly and asked with considerable irony: "Is that all you want, Father?"

The priest replied soberly—"That is all."—ignoring the irony. "Will you do it?"

Cannon shrugged, shaking his head with some puzzlement. "I don't know. I'll have to think on it."

He rose, shook the priest's frail hand, then opened the door and went through the dimly lighted church and out into the hot night air.

Automatically he fished in his pocket for tobacco and papers. The sounds of the night entered his ears but failed to register on his brain. He finished the cigarette but did not light it, distracted momentarily by the sudden, soft strumming of the same idler's guitar.

How long he stood there before the mission he did not know. He kept recalling the dim impressions of boyhood, the tobacco smell on his father's coat, the smell of horses. He remembered the little gifts of candy his father had sometimes brought him, and recalled being tossed high in the air by a black-bearded giant who laughed delightedly whenever the boy laughed. He even remembered going to sleep with his head on the rough woolen coat and wakening carefully tucked into his own bed.

Savagely he shook off these weakening memories. In a minute he'd be drooling mawkishly about character and innocence and good and bad like that priest back there.

All right then. He'd go to Red Butte. But he didn't have to like it and he didn't have to believe in what he was doing. All he had to do was to collar the old man and turn him over to the law. All he had to do was to save the old man's life.

Not from love, or duty, or even in respect. Not even because the priest had asked it so persuasively. But only because the old man was his flesh and blood—the last tie between himself and the old life—the one that had been so natural and so good.

★ ★ ★ ★ ★

In mid-afternoon of the third day, Stuart Cannon topped the crest of Comanche Pass and reined up in the timber to stare before him with a certain startled awe.

Below stretched the valley, bowl-shaped and nearly fifty miles long. The Giant's Graveyard, it was called, named for the dozens of strange rock formations that rose like tombstones out of the valley floor and towered 500 feet above it. Each was a straight-rimmed pillar of red sandstone that tapered off into a brushy, talus slope perhaps halfway down to the valley floor. They varied in shape, of course, and over the years each had been given a name. Red Butte. Seven Cities. Chimney Rock. Needle Rock. Elephant Rock.

Red Butte, the town, lay at the foot of Red Butte, the monument. Cannon's eyes picked it out at once from its remembered shape. It lay perhaps fifteen miles away, straight out toward the center of the Giant's Graveyard, partly obscured by a thin dust haze that lay unmovingly across the vast valley.

He twitched his reins, raising the horse's weary, drooping head, and continued downward until he reached the level expanse of valley floor. Then, with Red Butte to guide him, he pointed his horse out toward its center.

Nostalgic memories, stirred by the sight of the Giant's Graveyard, crowded Cannon's consciousness as he rode along and brought, inevitably, a return of his memory of that awful day, a return of bitterness.

He rode in a straight line, thoughtful and preoccupied, and near sundown found himself almost to the base of a monument called Chimney Rock and riding directly toward it.

Rather than detour its half-mile diameter, he rode up the talus slope on the eastern side, and at the top, backed by the bare, perpendicular face of rock, halted his horse to blow.

The sun, sinking toward the western horizon, had flooded the Giant's Graveyard with color. Red-orange tinged the bare faces of the towering monuments. Pink flowed across the sky. In the shadows behind the monuments, there was violet, deep gray-purple, and even a shade very close to green.

Movement on the valley floor caught Cannon's attention, and at once a more than passing interest stirred his face. He studied the rider below him briefly. Something else, farther away, drew his attention, and he discovered another rider a couple of miles away, approaching at a quickened gallop.

He returned his glance to the first rider with some puzzlement since it was that one who was behaving most peculiarly. He seemed to have no definite destination. Instead, he was circling and intently watching something as yet unseen by Cannon in the center of his circle.

Unable for the moment to see what the rider was circling, Cannon studied the man himself. Even at a distance of a quarter mile, he was plainly tall, plainly narrow-shouldered, and Cannon got the impression that he was rather on the unkempt side, although he could not have told why.

Cannon could not see his features at all, but he had another impression that was that the rider had something treed within that circle, something he had lately run to earth. There was a rifle in the man's saddle boot, its stock rising beside the saddle horn on the left side, and he wore a cartridge-studded belt and holstered revolver.

Cannon fished for makings and rolled a cigarette thoughtfully. Curious, he continued to watch.

Suddenly he caught a flash of gray within the circle.

24

Quite plainly the rider caught it at the same time, for instantly his revolver came out and fired.

A wolf, thought Cannon. And the man hadn't even touched it. Flat and sharp, the report reached Cannon's ears.

The gray shape faded from brush clump to brush clump, a shadow seen by Cannon only because of his greater elevation, but obviously unseen now by the rider who left his circle's perimeter and advanced toward its center at a gallop.

Cannon's forehead furrowed with puzzlement. How did it happen that the rider had managed to run a wolf to earth in country such as this? It should have been ridiculously simple for the wolf to elude him, and the animal showed no signs of being wounded. Even now, the wolf showed no inclination to run in a straight line, but continued to elude the rider by circling.

Then, quite suddenly, the rider did something strange. He returned his revolver to its holster and took down his rope.

Is he going to try roping that wolf? wondered Cannon in unbelief.

But it was becoming apparent that the rider could no longer see the wolf. It was becoming obvious that there was something else in the center of that circle. For the rider took a direct path to the center and his rope went out.

At a distance of over a quarter mile, Cannon heard a squall. There was a brief flurry of movement at the end of the rope. He heard the rider's laugh, taunting, cruel.

Cannon could see, at last, what the rider had caught. A man, an incredibly ragged, bearded man with gray hair that reached below his shoulders. A man with bare feet who whimpered and squalled like a wild thing, who fought the rope with insensate fury.

Recognition struck Cannon's memory like a blow. He knew the wild man, knew him from childhood.

He reined over unthinkingly and spurred down the slope. He had seen this cruel game played out before, although never quite so savagely, and never by grown men. He had even been a part of it once, and the memory of that stirred obscure shame in him.

Now, as he rode, doubt touched him briefly, and he questioned the wisdom of interference, but his doubt vanished before the continuous, animal-like squalling of the roped wild man.

III

Philippe Benoit. His story was legend in the Giant's Graveyard. Half owner of the sprawling Singletree Ranch, he had turned to a hermit's existence years and years ago after the death of his wife and infant child in the space of a few short months. Some said he had lost his mind. He lived in a tiny, one-room shack out in the middle of Singletree range, lived with his wild pets, and, if anyone approached, he'd flee into the brush, as timid as a deer.

As Cannon drew closer, he studied the man who held the rope's end. Wholly preoccupied with his cruelty, this man had no notice for anything but his helpless victim and did not see Cannon at all. He kept spilling Benoit, dragging him, laughing his high, thin, cruel laugh.

Cannon's first impression of the man had been largely correct. He was tall, gangling, and narrow-shouldered. Unkempt, too. His hair curled untidily at his neck and was long enough on both sides almost to cover his ears completely. His face was covered with a week-old stubble of mouse-colored whiskers. His nose was thin, with rather large, flaring nostrils. His lips were full, almost colorless, and slack and loose, twitching constantly.

Memory prodded Cannon as he watched the man, who suddenly looked up and met his gaze.

Cannon started. "Well, for Judas's sake! Turk! Billy Turk!"

Puzzlement touched Turk's wild, unstable eyes.

Cannon said with patent disgust: "Hell, I'd think you'd have outgrown this. Turn him loose."

He was unprepared for the violence that flared in Turk's eyes. And he saw no recognition of himself there.

At the end of the rope, Benoit gained his feet and clawed at the loop. Turk's glance flicked to him and he reined his horse aside to spill Benoit again.

But Cannon was in the way. Deliberately he had ridden up on Turk's off side and he stood his ground as Turk's horse collided with his own.

He was prepared for a fight, he was even ready if Turk had chosen to draw his gun. Instead, Turk did the unexpected. With a wild-eyed glare at Cannon, he sank spurs into his horse's sides.

The horse leaped out, in a full, hard run before he had covered a dozen yards. The rope jerked cruelly tight, dallied as it was to Turk's saddle horn.

Benoit screamed as the loop cut into his flesh, as the tightened rope yanked him off his feet. He fell into a clump of sagebrush, caught on its tough, twisted trunks, and flopped free like a rag doll.

Thought was not conscious in Cannon, but he was aware that Benoit would be a bloody, dead thing in a matter of seconds if something were not done.

The motion that brought his gun clear was automatic. It

leveled and barked. He holstered it and sank his own spurs even as Turk's horse faltered.

Dust raised in a cloud from Benoit's limp body. Dust raised from the hoofs of Turk's horse. The animal's head went down and his front legs collapsed beneath him.

With a saddle man's instinct, Turk's feet kicked free of the stirrups and his body went limp and relaxed. As the horse fell, he flung himself clear, aided by the horse's own forward catapulting movement. He landed a dozen feet away, head first in a clump of brush.

Recognizing the extreme danger that Turk would present once he collected his senses and gained his feet, Cannon kept going and jumped, running, from his saddle while he was yet twenty feet from the wildly struggling Turk.

Turk fought the brush savagely, trying to gain his feet, and he did while Cannon was still half a dozen feet away. Instantly Turk's hand flashed toward his gun.

Cannon hit him with all the drive of his running body behind the blow. He could almost feel Turk's nose split, and blood spurted out as suddenly as though Cannon had smashed a ripe tomato.

Turk lifted clear of the ground, went over the brush clump, and landed behind it. When he came up, his eyes were blinded with tears and his nose streamed a crimson flood.

Cannon scrambled around the brush clump and sank his fist in Turk's belly, getting a kind of savage pleasure from the grunt that escaped Turk's twisted mouth. He grabbed Turk's right wrist and whirled the tall man around with a vicious twist. He yanked Turk's gun from its holster and thrust it into his own belt. Then with a certain disgust, he flung the whimpering Turk away from him.

Breathing hard, he retraced his steps to the place where Turk's horse lay, utterly still on its side. He withdrew the rifle from the saddle boot, jacked the cartridges out into his hand, then flung the rifle into a thick clump of brush. He put the cartridges into his pocket.

With the wild flare of action over, he stood still for an instant, breathing hard. His knees trembled slightly and he could feel the nerves jumping all through his body. He remembered Benoit.

The brush was high here, higher than a man's head. He could not see Benoit from where he stood, but he could see his horse—and another horse that had not been there a moment ago.

He remembered the rider he had seen approaching at a gallop, and came around the clump of brush with a tense readiness within him. He relaxed instantly as he saw a girl, bending over Benoit's limp body.

She heard him, and looked around, her eyes blazing with outrage. She looked almost savage herself. Her glistening black hair tumbled across her face. Her dark eyes flamed. Her mouth was twisted with anger.

Puzzlement touched her at once as she saw Cannon: "Who are you? I thought. . . ."

"You thought it was Billy Turk? It was. He's over behind that brush with a bloody nose and a pain in his belly."

She seemed to forget him after that and turned back to Benoit.

The wild man's face was covered with brush scratches. His shirt had been torn almost off him, exposing a thick chest covered with gray hair. He was breathing, Cannon noticed.

The girl was wiping his face ineffectually with a scrap of white handkerchief. Cannon knelt and grabbed Benoit's wrist. The pulse was steady and strong. He examined the wild man's head, finding a rather nasty lump.

He became aware of an elusive perfume and looked up at the girl, whose face was no more than six inches from his own. "He'll come around in a minute. He's just knocked out."

"What happened?" Her eyes, so close to his, were wide, frightened, like the eyes of a startled doe.

Cannon settled back on his haunches. His hand moved automatically to his shirt pocket and he began to make a smoke. "Didn't you see it?"

She shook her head. "I was crossing a wash."

Cannon grinned tightly. "I saw Turk rope Benoit and start to drag him. I interfered. Turk kicked his horse into a run, dragging Benoit behind him. I knew Benoit wouldn't live long, so I shot Turk's horse."

The explanation seemed to satisfy her, but it did not kill the puzzlement in her eyes. "How did you know their names? You're a stranger."

Suddenly Cannon remembered this girl. He said: "I'm no stranger. You're Eve Redfern, aren't you?"

She nodded, her bewilderment increasing. Cannon said: "I've been gone for a long time. I'm Stuart Cannon."

He could see that the name was familiar to her, as it naturally would be. He could also see that she did not remember him personally. He said: "I was only twelve when I left. That was after. . . ."

She nodded vigorously. "I know. I remember now."

Her forehead was furrowed, and he knew she did not remember him. She only remembered the name, and the lurid scandal connected with it.

Benoit groaned, and her glance went instantly to him. The wild man opened his eyes, which were crazy with fear.

30

They calmed when they touched the girl, and he even smiled very slightly. Eve said soothingly: "You're all right now. It's all over."

Benoit's beard was filled with dust and blood. His face was dirty. He struggled upright, and squatted on his haunches. The vague, blank look returned to his eyes, the look Stuart remembered so well. He stared at Eve, and at Cannon, and got to his feet. Cannon thought: *He's going to run. He's going to run away.*

But Eve caught Benoit's arm. "Let me take you home on my horse."

Benoit shook his head. He whirled and started to trot away. But his leg folded beneath him and he fell headlong.

Eve uttered a small cry. Cannon said, looking at Benoit's leg: "Twisted it. It doesn't look broken. But he won't walk home tonight."

He walked over and got Eve's horse. He led the horse to where Benoit waited, sitting up, and between them they helped Benoit into the saddle.

Cannon had, for the moment, forgotten Billy Turk. An uneasiness made him turn and he saw Turk, mopping his nose with a bandanna, watching with vitriolic hatred. Cannon said harshly: "Start walking. You can come back for your saddle in the morning."

Turk didn't say anything. He was so wildly enraged that he couldn't. But his eyes promised Cannon many things, none of them pleasant. He turned and stalked away, limping slightly, in the direction of town.

Eve spoke behind Cannon's back. "He won't let Benoit alone. Every time he crosses Benoit's trail, he follows it. Today, I just happened to notice Benoit's tracks with horse tracks following and I guessed that Turk was after him again."

So far, Benoit had not said a word. It was as though he were mute, as though he could not speak. He kept glancing from Eve to Cannon and back again in the way of a wild thing. Suddenly he reined aside and drummed on the horse's ribs with his bare heels. The horse broke into a gallop, and in an instant was out of sight, hidden from the two on the ground by high brush.

Cannon asked: "Will his wolf follow him home?"

She shook her head. "No. The wolf won't follow horse tracks. But he'll get home sometime tonight."

"You want to go back to town, or after your horse?"

"You mean you'd let me have yours?"

Cannon shook his head. "I didn't say that. You'll have to ride double."

She gave him a look that was filled with suspicion.

He said shortly: "Never mind. I'll bring your horse to you here."

Before she could protest, he swung up and rode away, leaving her staring angrily after him.

He was vaguely angered himself. Why did women always have to think that every man they met wanted to get his hands on them? He'd only suggested riding double because it would save time and effort for everyone concerned. Now she could sit and wait until he was blamed well able to get back for her.

He picked up Benoit's trail without difficulty although the light was fading fast. And kicked his horse into a fast trot.

He thought he remembered where the Benoit cabin was, but it had been a long time since he'd been there and he knew there was a good chance of wandering around for hours without finding it. The simplest way, then, was to follow Benoit.

He hurried along and, as the first star twinkled in the deep-gray sky, came in sight of the shack that Philippe Benoit called home.

IV

There was a lamp burning in the dilapidated shack, shining out through the open door. Eve Redfern's horse stood motionlessly immediately in front of it, reins trailing.

Cannon wondered briefly, as he rode in, whether Benoit had a gun or not, but shrugged, knowing he'd have to chance that.

Fifty feet from the cabin, he hailed: "Benoit! I came for the horse!"

He had to grin as Benoit burst from the door and, limping noticeably, disappeared into the brush. From the direction Benoit had gone, Cannon heard a coyote bark.

Another of the old man's pets, he supposed, no wilder than the old man himself.

He reached the door, and would have simply snatched the trailing reins without dismounting except for the fact that he saw a man's booted feet and lower legs inside the cabin.

Curiosity touched him, for he could not imagine Benoit and anyone else sharing the cabin. He swung down from his horse and stepped inside.

A man lay face down on the filthy pile of blankets that was apparently Benoit's bed. Beside the man was an empty whiskey bottle, and the cabin reeked with whiskey that had spilled from the bottle and onto the blankets. From a barred cage on the far side of the room, a bobcat snarled and spit as Cannon came in.

For an instant Cannon hesitated. Perhaps he might have

turned and gone out. But at that instant he felt the vaguest sense of familiarity with the man on the floor.

The man was balding, and graying, too. But his hair had once been black, and his head had once been shaved.

Cannon stooped, suddenly enraged, and seized the man's shoulder. He yanked savagely, and the man rolled over onto his back.

As he stood, staring down, the years of hatred, the years of bitterness came flooding back, until it was all Cannon could do to keep from flinging himself upon the man on the floor. He had never wanted to kick anything so much before in his life. His face was white, terrible.

One of the man's boot tops had been cut away and his ankle was red and scabbed where the leg iron had been. His clothing was ragged and old, stolen no doubt from some Mexican hut near the prison.

There was no substance to his body, and the clothes hung upon it like sacks. His face was hollow, gaunt. He was drooling a little and his lips were slack, his mouth half open. He was dirty, unshaven, possessed of an unhealthy skin tone, caused no doubt by his years inside the dark prison.

But he was Stuart Cannon's father. In spite of change, in spite of Stuart's memory of a black-bearded giant, this was the one. The illusion of great size had been caused by Stuart's own small size.

A growl began deep in Cannon's throat. "Damn you! You killed my mother in a drunken stupor, then you get out of jail and the first thing you do is go into the same kind of drunken stupor!"

He was hardly aware of his surroundings, of the unutterably filthy cabin, of the crouched bobcat, watching him with yellow, unblinking, hate-filled eyes, of the smaller cages and their contents of small animals.

34

For he was thinking of Father Gonzales, of all those fine words about love and honor. He was thinking that here was the man who had broken prison because he could not stand the thought of his son hating him—that here lay the man who had risked his life to prove he was not guilty of the crime he had been convicted of. Drunk! Dead drunk!

Cannon's fists were clenched at his sides. His whole body was trembling with repressed rage.

How long he stood thus he could not have said. He was unaware of time, of its passage. He was unaware of everything but the man who lay snoring at his feet.

Some small part of his mind asked: *Well, what are you waiting for? You came to catch him, didn't you? You've caught him, haven't you? It was easy, but it was only luck, because neither you nor anyone else would ever have thought to look for him here.*

Benoit must be one of the friends the priest had mentioned. Cannon shook himself visibly. He felt almost physically sick. He stooped, controlling his revulsion with difficulty, and picked up the limp form on the floor. It seemed weightless in his arms, but there was no pity in him.

He carried the man out and flopped him across his saddle. Still unconscious, the man retched. Reaching up, Cannon looped the old man's belt over the saddle horn to hold him in place. He picked up the reins of Eve Redfern's horse and mounted his own animal, settling himself behind the cantle on the horse's rump. The horse didn't like it, but Cannon held him with a harsh hand.

His eyes were bleak, but surprise touched them as Benoit came timidly from the darkness. Benoit asked worriedly in a cracked, scarcely understandable voice: "Where are you taking him?"

"Red Butte Jail."

Benoit plainly wanted to protest, but the timidity of the wild was too strong in him, and, besides, there must have been something about Stuart Cannon's eyes and still face that stopped him.

Cannon reined around and rode away.

His thoughts were not pleasant, nor was his expression. Strong by necessity himself, he had no real understanding of weakness in others. He could not understand, for instance, how a man who has once depended upon liquor could crave it, even after ten years without it.

Cannon had never liked the stuff himself. He distrusted its effect on the sharpness of his mind, the sureness of his judgment. And he didn't like its taste. It gagged him. Perhaps there was also a psychological distrust of liquor in him because of its responsibility for the wreckage of his life.

Here, before him, was an example of what liquor could do to a man. In the saddle before him, Lloyd Cannon stirred, and groaned, and dry-retched again.

Full dark came down upon the land as Cannon retraced his way to where he had left Eve Redfern, guiding himself by the towering silhouette of Chimney Rock.

He rode to within 100 yards of where he had left her, and was halted by her hail, which made no attempt to conceal her anger and irritation. "Stuart? Over here."

He turned and rode directly to her. Without speaking, he handed the reins of her horse down to her. She made no attempt to mount, in spite of the impatience that had been in her hail. She was looking at the burden in Cannon's saddle, and at once a deep, frightened concern touched her voice: "Is he . . . was he hurt worse than we thought?"

Cannon said harshly: "This isn't Benoit. This is my father, Lloyd Cannon. He's drunk, Miss Redfern. Dead drunk. I'm taking him to Red Butte to jail."

"Where was he? Where did you find him?"

"In Benoit's cabin."

A certain incredulity touched her voice. "And you're going to turn him over to the law? Just like that?"

"It's what I came here for."

"But he's your own father! He risked his life to escape from prison. Aren't you even going to wait until he comes to and talk to him? Don't you care why he escaped? Don't you even care to know why his freedom was so important to him?"

Cannon laughed coldly. "I know what he claimed was his reason for coming here. He claimed he was innocent. He was going to find out who really killed my mother." There was a world of bitterness in Cannon. At the moment there was only bitterness—nothing else. "But he didn't believe it enough to stay off the bottle. So now he's going back to prison."

Eve Redfern hesitated for a moment, then mounted her horse.

Cannon said: "Lead out. I'll follow."

She did so, wordlessly.

For a while they continued to ride in silence. Finally Eve said: "You give me the shivers. How can a man be so cold, so heartless? Do you hate him that much?"

"I don't hate him at all. I stopped hating him a long time ago."

"Then why . . . ?"

Cannon said flatly, contemptuously: "He killed my mother. Am I supposed to respect him after that? How strong do you think the ties of blood should be? I told you I didn't hate him, and I don't. I just don't have any use for him. I don't want to see him and I don't want to think about him. I let myself be talked into coming here because the priest at the prison was afraid he'd be killed before he'd let himself be captured." Cannon laughed mockingly. "A kid could have taken him."

"Have you considered that your father might be telling the truth?"

Cannon growled impatiently: "You were a child when it happened. You don't remember. He was drunk that night just like he is right now. He didn't remember a thing. He didn't know whether he did it or not. But a jury said he did and they sent him to prison for life. He spent over ten years in prison. Then, all of a sudden, he decides he isn't guilty. So he escapes." He stopped, and then said shortly: "I don't want to talk about it."

Eve was silent for a while, but at last she said: "I remember you now. I think the reason I didn't before was that you've changed so much. You're not the Stuart Cannon I knew. You've spent your life brooding and hating until. . . ." She groped for words angrily. "Maybe you have stopped hating your father. But you hate everything else instead. You hate the world and the people in it."

"Do I now?" Cannon's own anger was on the rise.

"Yes, you do."

Cannon could not understand his own defiance. "And why shouldn't I? I've had to fight for. . . ." He stopped, chagrined at the way he had so nearly been drawn out. This girl would not understand his bitterness. She had no idea of what it was to fight for each mouthful of food, to be cold and hungry. She could never understand a boy's wish to be accepted, a wish forever answered with suspicion and abuse. She could not know how eventually a shell formed as a defense against that. A hard, impenetrable shell, so that the kicks and blows could not hurt so deeply.

Suddenly he wanted this to be over with—finished. He

wanted to be away from this girl, wanted to be rid of the inert burden in the saddle before him. He withdrew into a shell of taciturnity answering her conversational attempts with curt monosyllables, until at last she gave up angrily.

Thereafter, they rode in complete silence, until the lights of the town winked at them through the darkness.

To Stuart, riding in, the town seemed much smaller than it once had. The buildings seemed shabby, and the Southwestern Hotel, once so grand a structure in his eyes, was only an ornate, rather small two-story building badly in need of a coat of paint.

There was an odd, unpleasant feeling in his stomach as they passed the livery barn, so vividly did its unchanged appearance stir his memory. He said: "Is the jail still in the same place . . . a block south of the livery barn?"

"Yes." She reined in beside him and studied him. He found her regard disconcerting, and looked away. She said: "Won't you reconsider? Won't you wait and talk to him?"

"No." He didn't like uncertainty and he didn't like doubt. He liked things simple and uncomplicated, even his own thoughts and emotions. You were hungry, and you ate. You were tired, and you slept. You craved the company of a woman and you found one, but not one who would try to confuse you and make something binding and complicated out of it. Talking to his father could accomplish nothing.

He did not tell Eve Redfern good bye. He simply reined over and headed for jail.

V

Eve Redfern watched him go. There was considerable anger in her expression. She could not recall ever meeting a man who angered her so instantly, who kept feeding the anger within her so continually. *He's not a man,* she told herself. *He's a block of stone.*

Yet she knew, even as she thought it, that it was not true. He had simply built a wall of stone around himself and it was, perhaps, natural that the wall offered a not-to-be refused challenge to Eve. Walls were made to be breached.

She saw him rein in before the lamplight coming from the window of the sheriff's office, saw him shift the inert man in the saddle to his shoulder, and stride to the door. She turned her head away, frowning in a troubled way.

Eve Redfern was a beautiful girl. She was accustomed to being treated as such. This was a land filled with working men, with fighting men, and there were not enough women to go around.

It was not that Eve was vain. Actually she did not even enjoy the eager attention shown her by most men. But Stuart Cannon's cold indifference, by its very novelty, both intrigued and annoyed her.

Her horse stood patiently for a moment and, when Eve did not move, stirred and headed for the hotel automatically out of long habit. Eve let him go, reins slack.

She was a small, slight girl, filled with a boundless, nervous kind of energy. It showed itself in her quick, clean movements, so like the prancing of a high-spirited horse. It showed itself in the things she did to dissipate it—the long rides, the violence of her home activity when at times she would clean the entire house in a single day.

When she baked, she filled the kitchen with her baking,

and spent the following two days riding hither and yon giving it away to families in need. When she sewed, she did not rest until she had finished whatever it was she had started.

She was hard on horses because she was impatient, because in driving the horse she was, in a way, driving herself. Most times, in spite of her father's objections, she wore a split riding skirt of a length that would have been considered scandalous in any but John Redfern's daughter, and a small-size man's plaid shirt, the brighter the better. Her hair was long, an inky, silken mass, whose tumbling confusion so annoyed her that she wore it tied behind her head with a bright ribbon.

No amount of sun seemed able to darken her smooth, ivory skin, and the only evidence of her exposure to it was a small bridge of golden freckles across her nose. Her eyes were the green of jade, yet they had none of the coldness so common in green eyes. She resembled in no way the blond giant who was her father. And this was sometimes puzzling to her.

The town was rather quiet tonight. Riding along, she spoke to two or three people she passed, and their voices, answering, were friendly. She kept seeing that still, wary face of Stuart Cannon. She kept wondering what thoughts were behind its carefully controlled lack of expression.

Her anger came back, but this time, strangely enough, it was anger at herself rather than at him. *Forget him,* she told herself impatiently. *He's done what he came to do and he'll probably be gone before morning. You'll not see him again . . . and a good thing, too. He's unpleasant and cold, and probably a troublemaker as well.*

She dismounted at the hotel steps. From the verandah a Singletree cowpuncher came and took her reins. She murmured—"Thanks, Dutch."—smiled at him, and went on up the steps. Behind her, Dutch called in a softly warning voice: *"Viel Glück, Fräulein.* You vill need it. Your father has been for you vaiting already two hours."

She entered the tile-floored lobby and found him instantly with her glance. At the sound of the door, his ponderous head swung toward her.

He was scowling and red-faced. His hair was a good deal like a lion's mane, and there were times when his face had its own odd resemblance to that of a lion. This was one of those times. His pale eyes seemed to blaze at her.

She went to him and said quickly: "Father, Billy Turk was after Philippe again. He roped him and was dragging. . . ."

"I've told you not to ride after dark."

She ignored that. "Father, guess who's in town after all these years?" She was desperately trying to divert his thoughts from herself. Not because she feared his anger but because she wished to avoid a scene here in the lobby.

He growled disinterestedly, aware that he was being purposely diverted: "Who?"

"Stuart Cannon. I haven't seen him since he was twelve. His father broke out of prison and was staying at Benoit's place." Breathlessly she launched into a narrative of all that had happened that afternoon, accounting for her being late, and ending up with Stuart's delivery of his father to the jail.

"His father has come to the conclusion that he didn't . . . well, kill Stuart's mother. He came back to try and prove it. I think it's awful to haul him to jail, but maybe after Stuart talks to him he will believe in him, too, and try to get to the bottom of it for him."

She saw that she had succeeded in diverting her father's thoughts from her lateness. His anger had faded and the flush it had caused was gone from his face. He busied himself with a cigar that he took from the breast pocket of his coat. He unwrapped it and bit off the end. When he spoke, his voice was calm, almost without expression: "That's a sordid story for a young girl to be thinking about. You'd better forget it." He took her elbow. "Come on. I'm starving."

Eve could feel his hand trembling against her arm, but he seemed to have forgotten entirely her lateness and his anger because of it.

Usually he held her chair for her in his ponderously gallant way, but tonight he did not. Ruth Layton, the waitress, came at once with her deferent: "Good evening, John. What will it be tonight?"

And only after John Redfern had given his order did Ruth look at Eve. "Hello, Eve. You want the same thing?"

Eve nodded.

Redfern said: "Hurry it, Ruth. We're already late."

"Of course." Ruth hurried away, a thin, springy woman of middle age who never quite managed to conceal the adoration she felt for John Redfern but who never for a moment forgot its futility.

Eve noticed that her father still held the cigar, unlighted, in his hand. As she watched, he tucked it absently back into his pocket.

She asked: "Are you worried about something, Father?"

"Worried?" He shed his preoccupation instantly. "Of course not. Why should I be worried?"

"I don't know, but. . . ."

"Nonsense." He looked around the room. "Where the devil is Ruth? I'm hungry."

Ruth came threading through the tables, bringing their supper, and Eve attacked hers at once with a healthy, girlish hunger. She was not quite finished when John Redfern rose. "I have some things to do, Eve. I'll see you later."

He rose, smiled at her absently, and left the room. Eve glanced across at his plate and discovered that he had scarcely eaten a bite, in spite of his earlier statement that he was starving.

A puzzled frown drifted across Eve's smooth forehead.

VI

Upon leaving the dining room, John Redfern went out onto the hotel verandah. He fished the unlighted cigar from his pocket and studied it thoughtfully before putting it between his teeth and lighting it.

Dutch Vosmer, still idling in one of the cane chairs, spoke to him softly: " 'Evenin', Mister Redfern."

Redfern nodded. He stood there for almost ten minutes. Then, suddenly, his abstraction vanished and he said, turning toward Vosmer: "Dutch, find Billy Turk and tell him I want to see him."

"Sure, Mister Redfern." Dutch's voice, while courteous, showed no particular enthusiasm. Redfern turned and went into the hotel. He climbed the stairs to the small suite of rooms that was his home in town and, without removing his hat, crossed to the writing desk and sat down.

He selected a sheet of paper and with a pencil began to print carefully on it. When he had finished, he folded the paper, slipped it into an envelope, and sealed it. On the face of it, he carefully printed the name of the addressee.

He had scarcely finished when someone knocked on the door. Redfern stuck the envelope into his side coat pocket before he called: "Come in!"

44

Turk came in. He held his hat in his hands, and his face was a mass of brush scratches. His nose, normally straight and narrow, was swelled painfully, twisted, and varied in shades from purple to a dull green-black.

Redfern said: "I thought I told you to leave Benoit alone."

Turk's eyes flared. He didn't answer. His lips quivered sullenly and one corner of his mouth twitched. His eyes were bulbous, protruding, and one of them was slightly crossed.

Redfern did not make an issue of Benoit, being aware that he could no more keep Turk away from Benoit than he could keep a house cat away from a mouse. Instead, he said quietly: "There's something I want you to do. I want it done right and I don't want anyone to know you did it."

Turk made an obvious effort to turn his thoughts from their own channels, and in the attempt grinned rather vacantly and foolishly.

Redfern said sharply: "If you're caught, it's your problem, understand? Blab and you won't live to blab a second time."

Turk's grin faded before Redfern's intensity. Redfern studied him a moment. Turk was savage and vicious and he wasn't overly bright. It was always hard to tell what Turk might do. But there was a tenacious loyalty in him toward Redfern and Singletree, a loyalty that Redfern had inspired over the years by always getting Turk out of the scrapes his viciousness got him into. Redfern was reasonably sure he could count on Turk's loyalty in anything.

He said: "There's a man over in the jail . . . Lloyd Cannon . . . the father of the man you had your run-in with."

Turk scowled, and licked his lips, puzzled apparently at

what this was all leading up to.

Redfern opened the desk drawer and took out a small, nickel-plated .38. He said: "This gun can't be traced to me. I want Cannon to have it." He saw the instant refusal in Turk's eyes and his own glance hardened. He said: "This is going to hurt young Cannon worse than anything else you could do to him. Take my word for it."

"But how . . . ?"

"How are you going to get it to him? Very easy. You know that old woodshed behind the livery barn? Well, there's going to be a fire there in about an hour. It's almighty close to the livery barn, and, if the livery barn goes up, the whole town will, too. Everybody knows that, and everybody in town will turn out to fight the fire." He smiled a little. "There's no one in the jail but this Lloyd Cannon, and he's dead drunk. You be where you can watch the jail door. When the sheriff runs out, you go in, but be careful you're not seen. The sheriff's got an extra set of keys in the top left-hand drawer of his desk. Unlock Cannon's cell and slip the gun down inside his belt where he can't fail to find it. Then get out and don't forget to lock the cell door behind you." He could see questions forming in Turk's slow mind, but he gave Turk no time to formulate them. He said: "Don't forget, now. And no more drinking until you've done what I told you."

Turk nodded. He turned his hat around a couple of times in his hands, shuffled his feet, and cleared his throat. But in the end he decided against questioning Redfern and turned to the door. He went out without looking back, and Redfern crossed the room and closed the door.

He sat down, outwardly calm, and waited. He went over his plan in his mind, carefully scrutinizing it for flaws. If all went as he had planned it, Cannon would get the gun. The man from the prison would get the anonymous, printed note in Redfern's pocket.

Sometime tomorrow, when his hang-over had worn off enough so that he could think, Cannon would make his break. The man from the prison, warned, would be watching. He wouldn't know what he was up against, one man or a dozen. So when Lloyd Cannon ran out with a gun in his hand, the man would shoot him down. No one would know how Cannon got the gun. And with the old man dead, it was certain that his son would saddle up and ride on.

Pleased with himself, and smiling slightly, Redfern got to his feet. He went downstairs, through the lobby, and out to the street. Dutch Vosmer was sitting again in the cane chair near the door. Dutch didn't drink, so there was little he could do when he came to town except sit here and watch the town pass before his eyes.

Redfern nodded to him and strolled down the street. He often took walks after dinner, and he knew that, unless he was seen, no one would think to connect him with the fire. He took his time, stopping frequently to talk politics or weather or the state of the cattle business with some acquaintance.

But three quarters of an hour after leaving the hotel, he was a block beyond the livery barn, and for once was by himself.

He stopped and lighted another cigar. He puffed on it contentedly while he scanned the street. Satisfied that no one was noticing him, he turned unhurriedly off Main and headed for the alley that ran behind the livery stable.

He walked along it quietly but making no obvious effort to conceal himself. He came to the small shed and eased open the squeaking door.

Split firewood was racked neatly along one wall. Along

the other wall were sacks of grain and perhaps a dozen bales of spoiled hay that the stableman could not use as feed but would not throw away.

Careful of his clothes, Redfern yanked the wires off one bale and scattered its contents carefully about the shed. He laid a narrow trail of hay from the pile to the door and paused there to look at what he had done.

It was very dark, but not so dark that he could not see. Satisfied, he thumbed a match alight and dropped it at the end of the hay trail in the doorway. Before it could catch and make a noticeable flare, he stepped outside and closed the door behind him.

He returned along the alley by the way he had come, and went back to Main, hurrying just a little now. There was one more thing to do.

It worked out precisely as he had hoped it would. He was just entering the hotel as he heard the first shout.

He crossed the lobby and climbed the stairs. Outside, the bell in the church steeple began to *clang* frantically. Doors along the hallway opened, tenants looking out. One man asked: "What's going on?"

Redfern said: "Sounds like a fire alarm." He went quickly to his room, but he did not close the door. He could hear the hotel emptying, could hear the commotion in the street that always went with a fire. Fire was a terror to the people of a small town, because there was never any telling where it would stop.

He saw the man who had been sent from the prison pass his door, and this was what Redfern had been waiting for. Quickly he returned to the hall, closing his door behind him. The man, running, turned the corner at the end of the hall and disappeared.

Redfern took the envelope he had prepared from his

pocket. He went along the hall until he came to the man's room and, stooping, slipped it under the door. Straightening, he looked down the hall to be sure no one had seen him.

Then, smiling in an extremely satisfied way, he broke into a run himself, heading for the stairs.

He'd fight the fire with the rest of them, and he knew there'd be no particular difficulty in putting it out. The shed was small, and there were fifty fire fighters. But the fire would have served its purpose and there would be no one to point a finger at John Redfern. Except Turk and Turk knew better than to spill anything he knew.

VII

Stuart Cannon had just entered his hotel room when the fire broke out. He went to the window and peered down into the street. At once his glance found the glare, and he knew that the fire was in the little shed behind the livery barn.

How many times had he stood beside that shed, splitting wood and carrying it inside? How many times had he wished it would burn down? He smiled a little, remembering.

He considered going downstairs to help, but realized at once that there were too many fire fighters as it was. They'd be getting in each other's way without any help from him.

Yet an odd restlessness possessed him tonight, so he put on his hat and went out into the hall. The last of the hotel's tenants were pouring down the stairs as he reached them, and he recognized the ponderous shape of John Redfern ahead of him.

Redfern had aged somewhat in the time Stuart had been gone. There was a silvery sheen to his yellow hair that had not been there when Stuart left. Otherwise, he seemed much the same, huge, confident, arrogant. The big man of the community.

Cannon descended into the lobby and went to the big plate glass window to stare into the street. Only a part of his mind was upon the confusion there, the remainder being upon the thing he had done this evening, upon his father sleeping it off on his cot in one of the jail's aseptic-smelling cells.

There was no reason, he told himself, why he should feel so guilty. He had done what he had agreed to do. He had kept his father from fighting to escape capture, perhaps had even saved his life. But he also realized that he had not done quite all the priest had asked him to do.

This, then, was behind his feeling of guilt. He crossed the lobby and sat down.

Eve Redfern came into the lobby from the verandah. Apparently she had been watching the excitement from there, for her face was flushed, her eyes sparkling. She glanced at him, hesitated, and then came toward him. "Aren't you going to the fire?"

He shook his head. "Too many now. They don't need me."

Her eyes mirrored her instant thought: *And you don't need them.*

Cannon felt anger stir, so obvious was her thought, but he said nothing. Eve sat down on the leather-covered sofa beside him, perching on its edge. She asked: "Are you going to stay in Red Butte?"

He shook his head. "I've done what I came to do."

Eve's eyes flashed dangerously. She made a determined

effort to control herself. "Where will you go?"

He looked at her without friendliness. "Back where I came from. Colorado."

"A ranch?" she probed.

He shook his head with exaggerated patience. "I've been trapping wild horses on the Colorado-Utah border. In two years I've put enough aside to buy myself a small herd of cattle. In another two years I'll have enough to buy a ranch to run them on. Is that what you wanted to know?"

"There's no need to be so unpleasant about it."

Cannon wondered what it was about the two of them that always managed to make the sparks fly. *Steel against flint,* he thought, but that didn't satisfy him, either, for there seemed to be no hardness about this girl.

She said: "You'll never be quite satisfied unless you talk to your father. You realize that, don't you?"

She put to words the thing that had been bothering him. He knew that what she said was true.

He said reluctantly and sourly: "All right. I'll talk to him, if it'll make you feel any better."

She stared at him, and then got up. Her voice was level, tight. "Right now I don't care what you do. I was right this afternoon. You may not hate your father, but you hate the world and everyone in it." She seemed about to say more. She seemed about to launch into a tirade. She controlled herself with difficulty and flounced angrily away. She ran up the stairs, and disappeared from sight.

Cannon sat quite still, his eyes smoldering. He did not like the confused state of his feelings. He did not like the way Eve Redfern could upset him.

She was a beautiful, vital woman and as such stirred certain earthy desires in him. These he had felt before and they were familiar and well understood. Yet the things she made

51

him feel were more complex, and troubled him because he did not understand them.

Another man, confused and troubled as was Stuart Cannon, might have left the hotel, found a saloon, and proceeded to get roaring drunk. He'd have gotten himself into a good fight and, upon waking in the morning, would have felt released, and calm again. No such release was possible for Cannon, feeling as he did about liquor.

Moodily he rose and climbed the stairs to his room. He went to bed, but it was past midnight before he slept.

As always, he awoke early. He got up, dressed, and walked to his window to stare outside. The monuments of the Giant's Graveyard were visible, and the rising sun stained their eastern faces a brilliant pink.

Nostalgic memory stirred in Cannon, and the almost forgotten feelings of boyhood came back. He remembered the sharp, friendly aroma of coffee, the small sounds his mother made moving about in the kitchen, the promise and challenge that each bright new day could offer a twelve-year-old boy. He remembered the feeling of belonging, of not being alone.

Not often did these memories return, but when they did, their pain was almost physical. For the briefest instant, his remote eyes were soft, his still face expressive with loneliness. Then he remembered his father, and the jail, and his promise to visit and talk to him before leaving today.

The wary look returned to his eyes, the brooding expression to his face. He washed and shaved quickly, then stuffed his belongings into his leather saddlebags and left the room. He paid his bill at the desk and went into the dining room.

So early, the place was nearly deserted. In silence he ate

his breakfast, and, rising, went out into the cool morning air.

He had left his horse at the livery barn with a boy of perhaps fifteen. This morning, the boy was gone, and the grossly fat liveryman Cannon remembered came from the tack room as he opened the door.

Odd, how things never changed. Cannon cringed inwardly at the impact of the man's unpleasant little eyes. It was almost as though time had rolled back and he was again a boy, entering here for his daylight to dark stint of cleaning stalls and currying horses. He wanted to sink his fist into the stableman's fat midriff.

He said: "At least you haven't changed, have you, Dawson?"

The man made a bewildered effort to remember him.

Cannon said: "Stuart Cannon, damn you. I promised myself at least a hundred times that, when I was big enough, I'd take a strap to you the way you used to do to me."

Fear touched Dawson's eyes, and he took a backward step and laid his hand on the handle of a pitchfork. "Don't try it, Stuart."

Cannon laughed harshly. "Shut up and get my horse."

Motionless, Dawson stared at him, but in the end his glance wavered and fell away.

Cannon said: "Chestnut gelding. Fifth stall on the wall from the back door."

Dawson shambled away. After a few moments he brought Cannon's horse. Stuart Cannon flung up his blanket and saddle and cinched down. He could not resist flipping Dawson a silver dollar and turning away without waiting for change. He led the horse out, mounted, and rode away without a backward glance.

He knew he had acted childishly, but found that he didn't feel much differently about Dawson than he had as a boy.

The sun was up now, and the streets were beginning to stir with life. Stuart Cannon reached the jail, and was swinging his leg over to dismount as he heard the shot. It came from inside the jail.

He froze, still in the saddle. A shot inside the jail could mean but one thing—a break. And Lloyd Cannon was the jail's only prisoner.

Across the street, a man who had been lounging in the shadow of a cottonwood trunk stepped into the street, gun fisted. He had a lean, wary look to him with his flop-brimmed black hat and black coat. He looked like a manhunter. Stuart realized that the man's gun had more or less centered itself on him in the absence of a better target.

There was no further sound from inside the jail. Stuart swung from his horse and led the animal forward. Then he ducked around the horse and approached the door.

Lloyd Cannon, unshaven, dirty, and wild of eye, flung it open and stepped onto the walk. In his hand he held a small, nickel-plated revolver.

This puzzled Stuart Cannon. Why was that prison manhunter idling across the street this early in the morning, unless he had reason to believe there was going to be a break? Hell, the old man had damned near walked into a trap.

He looked at his father, then down at the gun in his hand. He said: "Know me?"

His father's eyes were vague, frightened, trapped. The gun had swung immediately to cover him, but it had no real steadiness.

Stuart said: "I found you out at Benoit's place and

hauled you in here last night. If you're going to shoot me, get it over with."

"I couldn't shoot you, boy. Lord, you've changed." Lloyd Cannon's voice was a cracked whisper.

Behind him, Stuart could hear the shuffling steps of the prison manhunter coming closer. The pair was sheltered behind Stuart's horse, but it was a meager shelter at best. Stuart said: "Get back inside. There's a man from the prison in the street with a gun in his hand."

His father looked up, saw the man for the first time. His gun hand dropped to his side and his shoulders slumped.

In the street, the manhunter's gun roared. The bullet smashed a window beside Stuart's head. He gave his father a shove and followed him inside.

With the heel of his boot, he kicked the door shut behind him. The sheriff sat in his swivel chair, tied and gagged. His eyes were virulent. Stuart walked over and removed the gag. He said—"Tell that damned fool in the street to quit shooting."—but the sheriff only licked his lips and mouthed his tongue, trying to restore its moisture.

Lloyd Cannon seemed to be in a kind of daze. He still held the little revolver, but he had plainly forgotten it. He made a helpless and pathetic figure.

Stuart said: "Get back in your cell, Pa. You stepped into a rigged game. What beats me is who rigged it."

The sheriff hadn't said anything. Stuart cut the ropes from his hands and the sheriff stooped and yanked the hastily tied bonds off his feet. He got up and pushed Lloyd Cannon into a cell, first taking the nickel-plated revolver out of his hand. He locked the cell door and heaved a long sigh. "Judas! That was a devil of a thing to happen to a man so early in the morning."

The manhunter kicked open the door and burst into the

55

room. The sheriff said: "Put that damned gun away. Everything's under control." He looked at the nickel-plated revolver, then at Stuart. "You slip him this?"

"No. And that's a stupid question. Would I haul him in to you last night when I didn't have to and then slip him a gun so he could get away again?"

"No, I guess you wouldn't." The lawman was tall, stooped, patient, his face wrinkled like old leather. Guy Kearns had been sheriff of Monument County for twenty years, and was the man who had arrested Lloyd Cannon, who had testified against him at the trial. Stuart had always felt a kind of respectful awe in his presence and he still felt it.

Stuart was scowling. It was as though he were in a long tunnel of utter darkness, as though he had always been in that tunnel. But right now, he could see the faintest glimmer of light ahead. He said: "Somebody slipped him that gun." He looked at the manhunter. "How'd you happen to be standing over there this early in the morning?"

The man fished an envelope from his pocket and handed it to the sheriff. Kearns read it, and passed it to Stuart. Stuart read it and passed it back. He said: "Somebody is scared. Somebody wanted the old man killed as he tried to break jail. If that had happened, I'd have ridden on and forgotten the whole thing."

Kearns grunted. "If I was you, I'd ride on anyhow."

"Uhn-uh. Now I'm curious. I'd like to know who slipped him that gun. I'd like to know *why*. I'll stay till I find out."

The prison man said: "I'll start back with him this morning. There's a stage out at ten."

Stuart looked at him briefly, then back to Kearns. He said: "Sheriff, I think you owe me something. I brought him in to you last night. I saved you a lot of riding, and maybe I saved you from dodging a few bullets. Make them extradite him." The prison man started to say something, but Stuart cut him off. "Sheriff, you could have been shot because somebody slipped Pa a gun. Don't you want to know who did it?"

"How will keeping him here help?"

Stuart shrugged. "I don't know. But I'll bet that whoever it was knows something about my mother's death. If Pa's here to question, we'll get to the bottom of it a devil of a sight quicker."

Kearns looked at him sourly. He shrugged his thin old shoulders and spoke with ill-concealed reluctance to the prison man. "Extradite him. I won't give him up."

The prison man began to argue with Kearns, but Stuart knew that once Kearns made up his mind nothing would change it. He walked over to the cell and looked at his father, surprised that for once he didn't feel anything in particular—no hate—no dislike—nothing. He asked: "Where'd you get the gun?"

Lloyd Cannon licked his lips. He rubbed a hand over his unshaven face. "It was stuck in my belt when I woke up."

Kearns was watching Stuart closely as he turned. Kearns was hesitating about something, weighing him, but at last he said: "You might learn things that you don't want to learn. Have you thought of that?"

Stuart stared at him incredulously. His anger leaped like a prairie fire. "What're you trying to say?"

"Well, when a woman's killed. . . ." The sheriff didn't finish. Something he saw in Stuart's face seemed to close his throat. He swallowed with difficulty.

Stuart said harshly: "That's a man in that cell of yours. He's spent ten years of his life in a stinking prison. Are you suggesting that, even if he isn't guilty, I should let him go back and spend the rest of his life there?"

The years of bitterness and hatred had been bad enough, assuming that his father was guilty of his mother's murder. If he was not, they would have been for nothing. If Lloyd Cannon had not killed his wife, and someone else had, then the guilt of whoever had was truly appalling. Someone had to pay—for a woman's death, for a man's false imprisonment for ten years, for a boy's lifetime of bitterness and hardship.

There was a kind of craziness in Stuart Cannon. He stared wildly at the sheriff for a moment, then stalked hastily to the door. He had to think. He had to think.

Behind him the sheriff called out something he did not understand. He swung up on his horse, and rode out of town at the wildest kind of run.

VIII

Stuart Cannon was not really aware of the horse under him, or of the miles flowing past. He was not aware of the horse's exhaustion until the animal nearly fell while jumping a narrow wash.

Shamed, he pulled the horse in and dismounted. He took off the saddle and began to rub the lathered animal down with the saddle blanket. But his mind was not on it.

His life as a man had begun when he was twelve, for it was then that he had been cut adrift. It had been nurtured on hatred, which had gradually faded to be replaced by a philosophy of withdrawal, of total self-sufficiency, of distrust of his fellow men.

Today, the foundations upon which he had built his life were crumbling. For if Lloyd Cannon were in truth innocent. . . . He shook his head confusedly.

He became aware of the sound of a horse's hoofs and looked up to see Eve Redfern gallop into sight. She rode directly to him and he knew she had been following him.

She started to dismount, but changed her mind. All her assurance seemed to vanish as she looked at his face. She asked timidly: "What happened? I heard that your father tried to break jail. I was heading for there when I saw you ride out. Your face was so terrible, I. . . ."

He tried to concentrate his thoughts on Eve, but he did not really see her. Yet there must have been some softening in his expression for she dismounted and came to sit beside him. He dropped his head into his hands, covering his face and growing tense.

He sat this way for a long time. At last he shuddered and looked at her. He asked: "What if he didn't do it?"

"Do what? What are you talking about?"

He told her about the attempted jail break, about the revolver, and about the anonymous note. He said: "That fire was set last night. It was set to give someone a chance to get into the jail and put that revolver in my father's belt. Someone is scared. And now they'll be even more scared."

"What are you going to do?"

His eyes were terrible. "Find him, whoever he is."

"More hatred, Stuart? Suppose you're wrong. Isn't it possible that one of your father's friends, perhaps Benoit, got the gun to him?"

"Then how about the note?"

"Maybe someone saw Benoit or whoever it was go into the jail last night. Maybe they wrote the note rather than to become involved. Or perhaps they didn't want to accuse Benoit."

He looked at her steadily. "Do you believe that?"

She shook her head. "No. I don't believe it. But it's possible."

He had to admit that it was. And it was a steadying possibility. It eased the shock of such sudden and complete reversal of his beliefs.

Automatically he fished for tobacco and made himself a smoke. He lighted it and dragged the smoke deeply into his lungs. He discovered that it was oddly comforting to have Eve here beside him.

He said bitterly: "If he isn't guilty, someone has a devil of a bill to pay."

She did not speak at once. When she did, her voice was soft, almost timid. "And what about the bill you owe, Stuart?"

He didn't pretend to misunderstand her. "Maybe I can pay part of it by finding the killer. I'll pay the rest after Pa gets out of jail."

He looked at her and there was a film of tears in her eyes. She whispered: "I'll help all I can."

"Why? Why should you want to help?"

She was instantly angry. Her eyes flashed and her lips tightened. She got to her feet and stood looking down. "Why do you have to be so darned suspicious? Why?" she mocked. "Why? Why? Do I have to have a reason except that you need help and I want to give it?"

He had never said—"I'm sorry."—in his life, and he could not now. He stared at her, and she stared back, and dislike crept into her expression.

Without another word, she turned and mounted her horse. Looking down, she said: "I'm sorry for you. Because there's something you just can't seem to learn."

"What's that?" He was angry, he discovered, as much at himself as at her.

"You get out of life exactly what you put into it. You get out of your relations with people exactly what you put into them. You have never put a single thing into either your life or your relations with other people. It's no wonder you've never gotten anything out."

His face stilled and his eyes blazed. Eve whirled her horse and rode away at a hard run, leaning low over her horse's withers, her midnight hair streaming out in the wind behind her.

In an instant she was gone from sight. Cannon stood up and kicked viciously at a sagebrush clump. He was filled with a consuming, helpless rage.

He looked his horse over and discovered that the animal was breathing quietly, that his hide had dried and cooled. He saddled and mounted. He yanked his thoughts from Eve with an effort, and concentrated them on the problem that faced him. He realized that he faced a blank wall. He had been twelve when he left Red Butte. He could know nothing of the conflicts and problems that its inhabitants had faced. He could remember who had been here at the time and that was all.

Another thought occurred to him, and for an instant the helplessness faded from his face. Someone had engineered that jail break out of fear. The jail break had failed. Therefore, would not that someone's fear increase as a direct result of the failure? And would not their increased fear force still another move?

He decided that it would. He pointed his horse toward town, but now he did not hurry, preferring instead to let his thoughts wander as they would.

John Redfern was in the hotel dining room with Eve when Dutch Vosmer came hurrying in with news of the jail break. His accent thickening with excitement, Dutch related all that had happened. Before he was through, Eve got up and hurried from the room.

Redfern watched her go, trying hard to control the panic that clawed at his mind. He had not foreseen this. He had been a fool, but he had not foreseen failure.

He got up, partly to avoid Dutch's scrutiny of his face, and headed toward the lobby with Dutch walking beside him and talking excitedly.

Normally Red Butte was a dull town, enlivened only by the once a month antics of Singletree's cowpunchers when pay day came. In the past week, however, and particularly last night, enough had happened to keep the inhabitants supplied with excitement for months to come. Firstly, news of Lloyd Cannon's escape had come, immediately followed by the arrival of the manhunter from the prison.

Then Stuart Cannon had ridden into town with the old man draped across his saddle. This morning the jail break. No wonder Dutch was excited. Too excited, Redfern hoped, to notice the whitening of Redfern's face, the tremor that shook his hands.

He went through the lobby and out onto the verandah. He stared into the dusty street. He saw Stuart Cannon pound out of town as though pursued by the devil, and five minutes later saw Eve leave the same way. Dutch still talked brokenly and excitedly at his elbow and at last Redfern said: "Shut up, Dutch. You talk too much."

Abashed, Dutch fell silent.

Redfern had not felt panic such as he felt today for years. He had grown sure and confident with the passage of time and, he realized now, that very confidence had betrayed him. He had planned well last night, but he had not considered the possibility of failure. Now Stuart Cannon would be suspicious, ready for the first time in his life to consider the possibility that his father was innocent of the crime of which he had been convicted.

But wait! Redfern frowned thoughtfully. Perhaps something could be salvaged out of the situation. Without too great a loss of prestige. Perhaps he might even be admired for what he had done.

He started to speak to Dutch, then changed his mind. He fished a cigar from his pocket and lighted it.

Stuart Cannon, he realized, still remained a problem. Unless. . . . He turned abruptly to Dutch. "Go on out to the ranch. Get Tom O'Dell and bring him in. I want to talk to him."

Dutch looked puzzled, but he did not argue. He headed for the livery barn. Redfern puffed furiously on his cigar for a moment, then tossed it into the street and headed for the jail and the sheriff's office.

He could bring this off, he knew. For he was the other friend of which the priest had spoken to Cannon. He was the other man who had visited and written to Lloyd Cannon over the years.

The street was dusty, the sun warm against his back. He nodded briefly to Dawson, the stableman, who stood, sweating and puffing, beside the livery stable door. Dawson said breathlessly: "You heard about the jail break, Mister Redfern?"

Redfern nodded. His nerves were jumping, but he guessed it wouldn't hurt if he showed a little nervousness at the sheriff's office. Anybody would be nervous, confessing complicity in a jail break.

He hesitated with his hand on the doorknob, then straightened his ponderous shoulders visibly and went in.

All was quiet here now. The sheriff sat behind his desk.

Back in the cell, Lloyd Cannon sat on his bunk, staring moodily at the floor. He looked as though he might have a headache, for he held his head in his hands.

Redfern cleared his throat. Guy Kearns looked up, his glance neither friendly nor otherwise. Neutral. He said: "Sit down, John."

Redfern sat down in the chair beside the sheriff's desk. He fished a cigar from his pocket, his hands shaking visibly. He said: "I guess I was wrong. When I think. . . ."

Kearns's voice was flat. "What are you trying to say?"

"Guy, I was the one who arranged for Cannon to get that gun."

Genuine surprise touched Kearns's face. "But why? Why the devil would you do that?"

Redfern flushed and smiled, blending exactly the right amounts of humble shame and stubbornness in the smile. He felt just a little proud of himself. "I was Cannon's friend, Guy," he said simply.

He heard the stir of movement in the cell as Cannon got up and came to the bars. Redfern turned and said apologetically: "Lloyd, it never occurred to me you might be hurt."

Kearns said sourly: "And I'll bet it never occurred to you that Cannon might shoot me, either, did it?"

"I knew Lloyd wouldn't hurt you, Guy."

"Well, I wasn't so damned sure when he put that gun on me this morning, shaky as he was."

Redfern said, with an air of plunging in to unburden his conscience: "I set the fire in the shed to draw you out of the jail. Then I sent Billy Turk into the jail to leave the gun with Cannon. I'll pay for the shed, Sheriff. But I guess I'll have to stand trial, won't I?"

There was a world of humility in Redfern, and it was, perhaps, this incongruous quality that seemed to confuse the sheriff. Kearns mumbled: "Well, I don't know. Let me talk to Dawson. I have an idea, if he could make a nice profit on that shed, he'd forget about preferring charges. But, damn it, Redfern, don't ever pull anything like that again. You ought to have your butt kicked."

Redfern stood up. He went to the bars and looked at Lloyd Cannon. "I'm sorry, Lloyd. I knew how bad you wanted to be free. I knew you wanted to try and clear yourself. I thought. . . ." He left the sentence hanging. He could see that Cannon was tremendously moved.

He went out into the street. He was still shaking, but it was a pleasant thing now, the nervousness of intense relief. He'd pulled it off. He'd made it reflect to his credit. He had them eating out of his hand.

Behind him the sheriff yelled: "Hey!"

He turned, the fear crawling in him again.

Kearns said: "Come back here!"

Redfern walked back to the jail. He hoped he didn't look as panicky as he felt. But the sheriff's next question relaxed him wonderfully. "What about the note?"

Relief sighed out of Redfern. He smiled. "Someone must have seen me, or Turk, or both of us. Maybe they didn't want to get involved, or maybe they just didn't want to accuse me. They used the note as a way out."

"A damned dangerous way out, if you ask me," Kearns snorted. But the explanation seemed to satisfy him and he went back into his office, grumbling under his breath.

Redfern returned to the hotel, painfully conscious of the tight wire he was walking. One misstep, one error. . . .

He thought: *I've got to work this out. I've got to get young Cannon out of town, one way or another. Because the longer he stays, the more dangerous he'll become.*

There were, Redfern knew, some loose threads lying

around. At any time, Cannon might happen upon one of them. There was Flora Curtice. There was Benoit.

Well, maybe Tom O'Dell would get rid of Cannon. At any rate, it was an angle worth trying.

Redfern entered the hotel and climbed the stairs to his rooms. He sat down beside the window and stared down into the street. Eve had not yet returned, probably would not for an hour or more. Redfern had no idea, of course, how far things had gone between her and Stuart Cannon. Not far, he judged. Still, it was obvious that Eve was attracted to Cannon. And if Cannon was not attracted to her, he would be a fool.

At any rate, there was enough between them to feed Tom O'Dell's voracious jealousy. Redfern began to smile. Let Tom O'Dell work on this damned Cannon kid. Redfern was willing to bet that when O'Dell was finished with him, he'd be eager to leave Red Butte.

In a man like Redfern, confidence was renewed with each new plan. It was part of his monstrous ego. He began to smile, and thought: *That's a fight I wouldn't miss for anything.*

IX

When Stuart Cannon got back to town, he went directly to the jail. His father was asleep in the cell, snoring softly. A young, fuzzy-cheeked deputy was holding down Guy Kearns's swivel chair, his feet on the desk. He looked up at Cannon, scowled, and said: "What do you want?"

"Where's the sheriff?"

The deputy said shortly: "Out. He told me to tell you something. He said he was going to turn your old man over to the prison authorities in the morning. He changed his mind about makin' them extradite him."

"Why?"

The man grinned tauntingly. "Ask him."

"All right. I will." Cannon was making an effort to restrain the anger this deputy's taunting manner had raised. "Where is he?"

"See him later. He'll be back here at six. Now get the hell out of here. I'm busy."

Patience was at an end in Cannon. He crossed the room with a rush. He kicked the legs of the swivel chair viciously and it spun, yanking the deputy's feet off the desk and spinning him helplessly. It rolled halfway across the room, Cannon following it. Every time the deputy spun to face him, Cannon slapped his face hard.

The chair stopped and the deputy came out of it, snatching for his gun. Cannon grabbed his arm and twisted. The deputy uttered a thin sound of pain and sucked in his breath. He tried to knee Cannon in the groin. Cannon stepped back and hit him flushly on the mouth.

The deputy went backward, smashing against the wall with a crash that dropped two pictures from their nails in the wall. They hit the floor and both frames and glass broke.

A trickle of blood came from the corner of the deputy's mouth. He was not much older than Cannon, but his maturing had obviously been slower. Cannon thought he was going to bawl. The deputy's lower lip twitched and his eyes were wide with fear.

Cannon said: "Don't get tough unless you're tough enough to back it up. Now, where's the sheriff?"

"Over at Flora Curtice's place."

"Where's that?"

"It's a little white house on the street behind the hotel."
The deputy licked his lips and made no move to get up.

Lloyd Cannon, awakened by the commotion, came to
the bars and looked at his son but he didn't say anything.

Stuart went out, his temper simmering. He rode toward
the hotel and turned the corner beside it. He noticed John
Redfern talking to a big, wide-shouldered cowpuncher on
the hotel verandah, but paid no particular attention until he
noticed that they were both looking at him, obviously
talking about him.

He looked away, his mind on the sheriff, and was almost
past the hotel when the big cowpuncher called: "Hey, you!"

Cannon turned his head. The man was approaching him
at a swift walk. Cannon reined in.

The man said shortly: "Get down." His belligerence was
plain.

Cannon shrugged and dismounted. He was a full head
shorter than the big cowpuncher and a whole lot lighter. He
wondered what this was all about. He asked: "Sure you've
got the right man? I don't know you."

The man said: "You will. I'm Tom O'Dell, foreman of
Singletree." His quarrelsome manner was puzzling to
Cannon.

Cannon said: "You wanted something from me?"

"Yeah. Stay away from Eve Redfern."

Cannon's eyebrows raised. He was getting a little tired of
hostility. His temper was crowding a ragged edge anyway
over the way the deputy had behaved. He asked: "You own
her?"

"Don't get smart with me, damn you! There ain't no
room in this town for a woman killer's kid. So get out, fast.
And you don't see Eve again."

Cannon's eyes flared savagely with pure fury. But still he

didn't move. He said softly: "I'm not leaving. And while I'm here, I'll talk to whoever I damn' please. So if you've got any chips, shove 'em into the pot."

He hadn't thought so big a man could move so fast. O'Dell stood with his shoulders hunched a little, his legs spread. He came uncoiled like a steel spring, and his beefy left hand came out and smacked like a sledge against Cannon's jaw.

Cannon's feet left the ground. He was flung backward like a limp rag doll. He went under his horse, but the animal was too well trained to spook. He simply side-stepped until he was clear.

The instinct of a freight-yard brawler made Cannon roll, made him get his belly under him. The world revolved around him. He struggled to his feet, crouching, instinctively covering the vital places with his arms and ready to roll with any blow or kick that came at him. He reacted as a hurt animal does, waiting for the return of strength and the will to fight.

But no blow came. He straightened, his head clearing. O'Dell stood in the same place he had stood before. He said: "Get out of Red Butte." Quite obviously he thought this fight was over. He was a tremendous, vital man who was used to ending fights with a single blow.

Cannon gusted: "Oh, no! Uhn-uh. Let's get our money's worth out of this."

He knew those words were foolish even as he uttered them. He had been hurt by that first blow of O'Dell's. In addition to that he was plainly outclassed, by weight, by reach, by strength. Yet he could no more have failed to utter them than he could have failed to get up.

His eyes sized up O'Dell in that instant while they stood facing each other. O'Dell was surprised and his surprise held him motionless for a precious instant while Cannon's head cleared.

Out of the corner of his eye, Cannon noticed the hasty approach of Redfern, of half a dozen others. Suddenly O'Dell became an object upon which Cannon could vent his frustration, his seething anger. He rushed, his arms working like pistons, smashing O'Dell's thick lips, his nose, raining upon his craggy brows. The very fury of his attack made O'Dell back step, off balance. Every ounce of power Cannon possessed went into a blow that sank into O'Dell's belly and drove a grunt of surprise from the man.

O'Dell doubled instinctively, his hands dropping to guard his mid-section. Cannon drove a savage right at his throat, which connected with a sound like that of a face being slapped. O'Dell's huge arm batted him away and Cannon staggered for ten feet, fighting furiously to regain his balance.

He knew a feeling of helplessness, of something closely akin to fear. He'd put everything he had into that attack and he hadn't even dented the big man's assurance, much less hurt him.

But he'd made O'Dell mad, and at least that was a step in the right direction. He approached O'Dell warily, knowing he had to dodge the meaty impact of those beefy fists or be beaten in a matter of seconds.

O'Dell threw a whistling right that would have put Cannon out for half an hour. Cannon saw it coming, and for an instant thought he was too late to avoid it. O'Dell was fast, too damned fast for such a big man. Cannon's head came under the blow barely in time and it knocked his hat flying and grazed his head.

He countered instantly from his crouched position. He came up, using the rising drive of his legs, the power of shoulder and arm. His fist cracked against O'Dell's jaw with a shock that traveled clear to his knees.

O'Dell took three backward steps. His eyes blanked for the barest instant and his hand came up to rub his jaw. Cannon followed him, again raining blows into his face, blows that were largely wasted on the hand with which O'Dell now covered his face.

O'Dell backed another two steps with surprising quickness, and now both his fists swung wildly with a rhythmic flailing that Cannon could not for the life of him avoid.

A left against his shoulder drove him sideways, directly into a powerful, whistling right. And for the second time, his feet left the ground. He hit the dusty street sliding, doubling even as he struck. He rolled, and came to hands and knees, his head hanging stupidly as for the second time he waited for the numbness to clear from his head. A brackish taste was in his mouth, a burning blindness behind his eyes.

He heard the shuffling approach of O'Dell, sensed the savage kick aimed at his belly. He flung himself away from the kick even as it connected, and, while it sent him rolling again, the force of it was largely lost. Even so, it made sharp pain shoot from his ribs into the pit of his stomach.

He gained hands and knees again, his head clearing. O'Dell stamped viciously at one of his hands, and Cannon yanked it away a split second before O'Dell's boot came down.

His head was clearing rapidly now, and, as it did, a kind of wildness ran through him. He drove his body upward against O'Dell's legs and felt them give, felt the man begin to fall. O'Dell sprawled across him, and Cannon's rising movement flipped him over onto his back.

Whirling, Cannon came down with both knees into the big man's belly. The heel of his hand came up against

O'Dell's bony jaw, with Cannon's falling weight giving it force. O'Dell's head, which he had raised several inches off the ground, banged back against it with a sound like a meat cleaver hitting the block. And for the second time O'Dell's eyes blanked.

Cannon came to his feet. His lungs were afire with their gasping need for air. His chest worked like a bellows, and the sound of his breathing was harsh and raspy, almost like sobbing.

Panic touched him as O'Dell began to rise. Beating O'Dell was like trying to split a granite boulder with a tack hammer. He'd thrown everything he had at O'Dell and he hadn't hurt the man as much as O'Dell's first blow had hurt him.

Yet there was no retreat in him and no real fear. This was an old story to Cannon, who had beaten and been beaten countless times before.

O'Dell squatted, shaking his massive head stupidly. His lips were swelling, and blood ran freely from his nose. His eyes were red-rimmed, filled with a terrible fury. They were the eyes of a trapped, tormented wolf, of a hate-mad boar hog.

A low growling came from O'Dell's throat. He shook his massive head and struggled to his feet. He shambled toward Cannon, weaving a little, arms hanging straight down at his sides.

Cannon's next blow was a long shot, whose chance of success was slim. He drove himself forward, knowing he could break his hand on that massive, bony jaw, but knowing, too, that he had to have more force behind it than arm and shoulder muscles could give.

His legs were like pistons beneath him, driving him into motion, making his body surge forward. With all the weight of his driving body and its momentum, with all the powerful thrust of shoulder and arm behind it, his fist drove at O'Dell's jaw.

Pain shot through his hand and forearm as it connected. Shock traveled to his shoulder and numbed it. It was like hitting a stone wall with every once of power he possessed.

It stopped O'Dell, but it did not drive him back. Cannon ducked away, aware that his hand was probably broken, sure that he'd not hit O'Dell again with it in this fight. He knew he was finished, if O'Dell was not. The man could cut him to pieces now, in his own good time.

But Cannon had underestimated the terrible force of the blow he had just landed. O'Dell stood still, his eyes glazed, his jaw hanging slack, as though unhinged. Suddenly those terrible, red-rimmed eyes rolled upward, and O'Dell's knees seemed to turn to jelly. He folded to the street without a sound, sending little devils of swirling dust upward.

Cannon stood quite still, unbelieving, for a long, long moment. He heard the startled, awed talk that ran through the ranks of spectators. He knew he had been lucky, that except for chance it could well be himself instead of O'Dell lying there in the street. He also knew he'd have to face O'Dell again, and that next time the end could be quite different.

Tiredness weighted his body. His lungs, starved for air, worked like a bellows and his breathing made a whistling, sobbing sound. But, miraculously, he felt light and free. Bitterness had worked itself out of him during the fight. He found that he was grinning, although it hurt his jaw to do so. He looked around at the still-faced crowd and said breathlessly: "Anybody want to take it up?"

He got no answer, had expected none. Bravado had

Lewis B. Patten

made him ask, but he knew he couldn't have whipped that
fuzzy-cheeked deputy right now. He retrieved his hat,
walked to his horse, and picked up the reins.

So leaden were his muscles that he wondered if he could
mount. He grabbed the saddle horn, put foot in stirrup, and
gave a mighty heave. He felt the saddle smack him.

The air was cool and sweet and good, flowing in and out
of his lungs. He looked at Redfern, was surprised at the
man's expression. There was astonishment in Redfern that
the unbeatable O'Dell had been beaten. There was anger
that it could have happened. And there was something else
that looked like panic, or fear.

Cannon nudged his horse and rode away at a quick trot.

X

He reached the corner before he remembered where he
had been heading when the fight started. He looked for the
white house, spotted it, and headed toward it urging his
mount gently.

It was a neat, small house, well cared for, recently
painted. It had a white picket fence around its well-kept
front yard, and an iron hitching post whose top was a cast
horse's head. A horse was tied there and Cannon dismounted beside it and tied his own.

He kept trying to recall why the name of Flora Curtice
had been so familiar to him and finally grasped it, recalling
the snickers her name had always been able to start among
a group of boys at school.

The house, then, was an incongruity. There must have
been changes, in Flora Curtice as well as in the attitude
of the town toward her. In the old days she'd lived in a

shack out at the edge of town.

Cannon rubbed his jaw. It was sore, but he realized suddenly that O'Dell hadn't put a visible mark on him, save for a slight skinned place on the side of his jaw.

He mounted the steps and knocked on the door. An attractive woman in her early thirties answered the door. She looked at him questioningly.

Cannon remembered her as a blonde, but she was not blonde now. Her hair was warmly brown and was done in a restrained way with a bun low on the nape of her neck. She looked like any attractive wife might look and there was nothing about her reminiscent of her past.

She asked: "Yes?"

Cannon cleared his throat. "I'm looking for the sheriff. I was told I might find him here."

She smiled then, and her smile was quite warm. "Yes. Won't you come in?"

Cannon opened the screen door and stepped inside. Kearns sat on an upholstered horsehair sofa, and he looked rather startled as he saw Cannon. He scowled and asked abruptly: "What do you want?"

Flora Curtice looked first at Cannon, then at the sheriff. She diplomatically left the room and went into the kitchen.

Cannon said: "Your deputy said you'd changed your mind about making them extradite Pa. Why?"

Kearns straightened and sat on the edge of the sofa, elbows on knees, hands clasped between them. He said: "Redfern admitted to gettin' that gun to Lloyd. Said he did it out of friendship. It puts a different light on things."

Cannon was shocked, there was no denying it. He had made his mind up that a doubt as to his father's guilt existed, a hard thing for him, and now that doubt was being swept away. He asked: "What about the note?"

Kearns shrugged. "Somebody must have seen Redfern start the fire, or seen Billy Turk going into the jail. Redfern figures whoever it was didn't want to get involved, and wrote the note to avoid it."

"Then why wasn't the note addressed to you? You could have taken the gun off Pa before he got a chance to use it."

Kearns shrugged.

Cannon thought he detected resistance in the sheriff. He went on: "It's a nice, pat explanation, isn't it?"

"What're you tryin' to say?"

Cannon felt his anger stirring. "Suppose it was Redfern that wrote the note? His nice, pat explanation wouldn't do much good, would it?"

"I suppose not. But. . . ."

Cannon interrupted: "Redfern just sicced his foreman on me. O'Dell told me to get out of town."

Kearns started. "Then better git. He'll beat daylight out of you. . . ."

"He tried."

Kearns sat up straight. He studied Cannon closely, showing plain unbelief. "You mean you've had a fight with O'Dell?"

Cannon nodded. He rubbed his jaw.

"And that's the only mark on you?"

"Except for skinned knuckles." He flexed his right hand, deciding now that it was not broken. If he could move it, it couldn't be broken.

Kearns stood up abruptly. "This is something I've got to see. Where's O'Dell now?"

"He was lying in the street at the side of the hotel when I left him." Cannon would not have been human had he not felt a certain triumph in the telling.

The sheriff grabbed his hat, threw a look at Cannon, and

76

slammed out of the house. Flora Curtice came from the kitchen, and immediately, from the look on her face, Cannon could tell she had been listening. Her face was paler than it had been before and her eyes were no longer warm. She asked quietly: "You're Lloyd Cannon's son?"

He nodded. He looked at her for a moment, then he asked: "Are you ill? Hadn't you better sit down?"

She shook her head numbly. Her skin had lost all color and she looked as though she were going to faint. Cannon wanted nothing so much as to get out of this house.

He started to turn, but stopped as he heard her voice, very faint and low-pitched: "Why are you here? Why did you come back?"

Cannon said: "Pa escaped from prison. The priest at the prison asked me to come back and try to find him."

"Why?"

"The priest was afraid he'd be killed before he'd let himself be captured."

"What are you going to do now?"

It was a question that Cannon hadn't even asked himself yet. He didn't know. What he did know was that he wouldn't leave town in the face of O'Dell's threat and ultimatum. He said: "I'll stay a while, I guess. Pa seems to have gotten the idea that he didn't do it. Maybe I'll stay and see whether he's right or not."

Flora Curtice was showing a lot of interest, he thought, and she was behaving strangely. Her eyes were fixed on his face, filled with something resembling terror. He wondered if she knew anything, and, if she did, if she'd tell him what it was. He doubted it. If she had remained silent all these years, she probably wouldn't change now.

He said: "I'll be going, ma'am. You'd better lie down a while until you feel better."

"Thank you." Her eyes clung to him.

He wanted to shout: *What's the matter with me? Why are you looking at me like that?* But he clamped his jaw shut and went to the door. He looked back once as he went out. She had not moved, nor had her eyes left him.

He stood for a moment on the porch, aware that something was happening to him, but not understanding it at all. Then he turned in an abrupt rush and went back into the house without knocking.

Her wide eyes, in which such sudden terror leaped, confirmed his suspicions. He grabbed her by the shoulders and shook her fiercely. "Hang you, you know something! What is it? What are you so blamed scared of? You're not sick . . . you're scared because my name's Stuart Cannon."

"No! No! It's not true!"

"It is true!" Cannon could hear her teeth chattering. He said: "When I was a kid, you had a shack down at the edge of town and nobody in town would have anything to do with you. Now you're uptown and living in a nice house. It adds up to only one thing . . . blackmail. And it adds up to something else because there's only one man in this county with enough money to give you all the things you've got . . . John Redfern. He engineered a jail break to try and get my father killed. Has it occurred to you how dangerous it is for him to let you live? Particularly if I let the word get out that you've promised to tell me everything you know?"

"You wouldn't!"

"I would. Unless you open up and tell me what he's paying you for." Cannon couldn't quite conceal the triumph he felt at the success of his wild guess.

He was ashamed of what he'd done to her—until he remembered that this woman had allowed his father to spend his life in prison when a few words from her would have freed him.

She said: "Redfern was in your house when your father came home that night. I was . . . I was standing in a doorway across the street with a man. I saw your father come home. He had been out of work for a long time and had got to drinking and he was drunk that night. He staggered against the fence and passed out, hanging over it. Redfern came out and carried him into the house. He came back out and he happened to see me as he went by. The man I was with had seen none of it because he was facing me and because his mind was on me, but I'd seen it, and Redfern knew I had. When the news got out next morning, Redfern came to see me and threatened me. He said your mother was still alive when he left, but that it would ruin him if it was known he was there. So I agreed to keep still."

"And that's all?" Excitement was rising in Cannon. When she nodded, he knew she had told all she knew.

"You'll be quiet about what I've told you?" Her terror was pitiful. Cannon nodded.

He went outside and headed for the jail. He thought: *Why? Why? What did Redfern have against my mother?*

He met Kearns returning along the street. In the sheriff's eyes was a kind of unbelieving respect. "I wouldn't have believed it, Cannon. I wouldn't have believed you could do it."

Cannon shrugged. "Never mind that. Just tell me, what connection did my mother have with Redfern? You were here then. You ought to know."

The sheriff looked puzzled. "None that I know of." He shook his head. "Only time she had anything at all to do with him was the time his wife had Eve. Your mother went

79

out there to help because the doctor was away."

"And that's all?"

"All I know about."

Cannon frowned. "Thanks," he grunted and moved away, thoughtful and preoccupied. It didn't add. There seemed to have been nothing between Redfern and Cannon's mother that would have been strong enough to provide a motive for murder.

How about Benoit? He had been there at Singletree then. Maybe he'd remember something. Or perhaps Lloyd Cannon might remember something, if properly prompted—something his mother had said, perhaps some worry she'd had.

He remembered suddenly that he had forgotten his horse and returned along the street to where it was tied before Flora Curtice's house. He untied the animal and mounted.

Bitterness and hatred, stored over the years, had built up a bank of debt that nothing but a lifetime could repay. Cannon was suddenly aware of the debt he owed Lloyd Cannon, of the debt this town owed, too. He rode to the jail at a fast trot and dismounted before it. He went inside and looked across at his father, sitting dejectedly on the rumpled cot.

The downy-cheeked deputy scrambled to get his feet down off the desk. His eyes were wide, uncertain.

Cannon said: "Get out of here. I want to talk to him."

The deputy started to bluster, his jaw firming out. Then, because Cannon's gaze rested on him so harshly, and because he remembered the last time he'd gotten smart with Cannon, he said uncertainly: "You'll get me in bad with Kearns."

"The devil with Kearns. Take your keys with you if it'll make you feel any better."

The deputy went out and sat down on the bench in front of the jail, turning his head so he could see what was going on through the window.

Stuart picked up a chair and carried it over to Lloyd Cannon's cell. He looked at his father, wondering how he could ever have thought of Lloyd Cannon as a black-bearded giant. His father was not even big, even though he was a little taller than Stuart himself.

Lloyd Cannon got up from the bunk and shambled over to the bars, his face holding nothing but defeat, and a pitiful sort of eagerness. He'd given up hope of proving himself innocent. The eagerness, Stuart knew, was only eagerness for a little kindness from his son.

For some reason Stuart's eyes burned and his throat felt sore. He coughed and said: "You didn't do it. I know you didn't. I can't prove it yet, but I will. And then this town is going to make up to you all the years you spent down there." He drew in a deep breath. "I'm going to try making it up to you, too."

There wasn't much expression on Lloyd Cannon's face. But his eyes were awfully bright. He gripped the bars and his knuckles turned white. He was shaking all over. He croaked: "You've nothin' to make up, boy. The years ain't been easy for you, either."

There seemed nothing between them, nothing to make talk about. Prison had left its mark on the old man. It hadn't hardened him. It hadn't coarsened him. It had only bewildered and confused him. He lived now in a world all his own, where hurt and pain and regret were dimmed by distance. He tried to grin at his son and failed miserably. Then, because he couldn't seem to decide what to say or do, he shrugged and returned to his cot.

Stuart went outside. The deputy looked up at him and,

without saying anything, got up and went back inside. Stuart rode down to Main and turned toward the hotel. He saw a woman, skirts lifted, climbing the steps to the hotel verandah, and at this distance she looked like Flora Curtice although he couldn't tell for sure.

Pressure troubled him. He knew what it was, but he didn't know what to do about it. Lloyd Cannon had only until tomorrow, when the prison guard would start back to the prison with him. Somehow Stuart couldn't stand the idea of his father's returning to prison at all—at least until this thing was cleared up once and for all.

All right. Benoit was the last chance. His thoughts told him: *Get the devil out there and find out what Benoit knows. Even if you have to choke it out of him.*

Too many people hereabouts had been willing to let an innocent man go to prison. Too many people had been afraid, or greedy, and Lloyd Cannon had paid the bill. It was time someone paid him back. . . .

XI

Riding out toward Benoit's shack, Cannon kept mulling the puzzle over in his mind. There had to be a connection between Martha Cannon and Redfern. There had to be a connection that would provide a motive strong enough for murder. And yet what possible motive could there be for Redfern to kill a woman who had simply helped out while his wife was having her child? And how could such a motive carry over until ten or twelve years later?

If there was an answer, Benoit would have it, for he had been at Singletree when Eve was born. In fact, if Stuart remembered the stories he'd heard as a boy, Benoit's wife had

had a child at about the same time, a child that died.

Despondent over the loss of her firstborn, and perhaps unbalanced to some degree as well, Benoit's wife had killed herself. It was what drove Benoit mad, folks said, if he was mad.

Unable to put the puzzle together with so many pieces missing, Cannon dismissed it from his mind. He began to think of Eve, and there was a certain longing in his thinking.

Eventually he brought Benoit's shack in sight, and rode up to it openly, thankful now that he had intervened in Benoit's trouble with Turk a couple of nights ago. Perhaps there would be enough gratitude in Benoit to make him willing to talk.

Stuart hailed the shack, and Benoit came to the door, the wolf leashed at his side. Cannon could see the old man's fright fade as recognition came to him.

Cannon said: "I'd like to talk to you. I think I can clear Pa if you'll tell me all you know about Redfern and my mother."

A curtain seemed to drop over Benoit's eyes. He stooped and released the wolf, which darted at once for the brush. Cannon's horse must have gotten a smell of him, for the animal began to buck savagely.

Cannon rode him out and, when he was again able to control the animal, dismounted, and tied him securely to a clump of brush.

Benoit stood aside to let him enter. The rank odor of confined animals struck Cannon, and he said: "Let's talk outside. Those blamed cats make me nervous." He squatted against the wall of the shack and rolled a cigarette. He said: "There's someone in town who saw Redfern come out of our house the night my mother was killed. My father

83

came home about the same time and passed out, draped over the fence. Redfern carried him inside, and then came back out himself. I've got reason to believe that Redfern might have killed my mother and that Pa's spent all these years in prison for something he didn't do. But I can't think of any reason Redfern might have for killing her. Can you?" Stuart went on: "Near as I can find out, the only time Redfern had anything to do with my mother was when his wife had Eve. You were at Singletree then. Did anything happen that might give him a reason to hate my mother?"

Again Benoit shook his head, but now there was pain in his eyes.

Cannon said quickly: "Didn't your wife have her child at about the same time?"

Benoit's muscles gathered. He started to run, but Cannon's hand came out and grasped his ankle. Benoit fell headlong, kicking to be free. Cannon held on. He said: "Damn you, I helped you out the other night when Turk had a rope on you. You're going to help me out now if I have to sit on you till you do." Benoit's struggles stopped, but Cannon did not release him. Cannon said: "Didn't she?"

Benoit nodded.

Cannon asked: "How near the same time?"

Benoit's voice was a croak. "Same day."

"Wasn't that kind of queer? Two women having babies the same day?"

Benoit shrugged. "They were not supposed to. Your mother was out at Singletree to help my wife have her child. Missus Redfern's was not expected for another month. But she fell downstairs, and the child was born too soon."

"But it was your wife's child that died?"

"Yes." Cannon saw suddenly that Benoit understood

what he was getting at. Cannon felt sure he was on the track of something now. He asked urgently: "Who was with your wife and Missus Redfern when they had their babies?"

"Just your mother. The doctor was away from Red Butte."

Cannon knew he was guessing, but he said: "Suppose it was not your daughter at all that died, but Missus Redfern's? Isn't that logical in view of the fact that she fell downstairs? And suppose that Redfern bribed or persuaded my mother to exchange them?"

There was a dead silence while something wholly wild and unmanageable was born in Benoit's expression.

Cannon went on hastily: "Wait. Don't jump to conclusions. Let's work this out."

Benoit said: "You can let me go. I will not run away."

Cannon released him. He spoke in a soft, almost musing tone. "Mother took his money, maybe because she needed it badly. She went back to town. Then your wife killed herself, and you turned kind of wild. Mother probably blamed herself for your wife's death, for your condition, too. The years passed, and the load of guilt got too heavy to carry. Maybe she told Redfern that she was going to tell. Now what would you do in a fix like that if you were Redfern?"

"Not what he did!"

Cannon got to his feet. "I'm going back to town. You coming?"

Benoit nodded.

"Want to ride double?"

"No. I'll run along beside you."

Cannon untied his horse and mounted. By the time he kicked the horse into movement, Benoit was already 300 yards away in the direction of Red Butte. Cannon ranged up alongside of him and drew his horse into a trot. Benoit kept up, running tirelessly the way a wolf or a dog runs. His bare feet made a gentle, padding sound.

Cannon wanted to spur his horse into a wild gallop, but he restrained himself. He had until tomorrow. Lloyd Cannon was not due to leave for the territorial prison until then.

"There might have been a good many reasons for Redfern exchanging the babies," Cannon said as though thinking aloud. "One might be that he didn't want his wife blaming herself on account of that fall. Maybe that was the only reason. But after your wife killed herself and you left Singletree, he probably got so he liked running it all by himself. He probably got attached to Eve, too, and didn't want to lose her. He knew, if my mother talked, that Eve would hate him and that you'd come back to take over your part in managing the ranch. Besides that, he'd be forever disgraced in the Giant's Graveyard. He'd lose the position he values so."

It all fitted, thought Cannon. It fitted almost too perfectly. But it was the only explanation that did fit.

He didn't know quite what he intended to do. He only knew that he had to face Redfern, to accuse him. He'd know from the expression on Redfern's face whether he was right or not. After that, he'd have to play it by ear. It would be up to Redfern how it went from there.

XII

It was late afternoon when Benoit and Cannon reached Red Butte. Cannon reined in before the livery stable. His horse was tired and he knew the animal had earned a rest and a feed of grain. He looked at Benoit, whose only sign of his long run was his soft, even panting. "Wait here a minute. I'll put my horse up and then we'll go see Redfern together."

Benoit nodded, and leaned against the wall of the stable. His wildness seemed to have left him altogether. There was no blankness in his eyes, no apparent fear of the town or the townspeople. Yet there was another expression in his eyes that troubled Stuart, for it seemed unmanageable, unpredictable.

Stuart led his horse into the cool, shady livery barn and slipped off the saddle. He rubbed the animal's sweaty back with a gunny sack. Then he led the horse back to the same stall he'd had last night and dumped a generous measure of oats in the feed box. Leaving the horse quietly feeding, he went outside.

It was the supper hour, which explained the absence of an attendant at the stable. It also explained the absence of townspeople on the street.

Cannon looked around for Benoit, but Benoit was gone.

A vague uneasiness stirred in Cannon. *Why the devil couldn't Benoit have waited? And where could he have gone?*

Cannon remembered the unpredictable look that had been in Benoit's eyes, and began to walk at a fast pace toward the hotel. There was only one place Benoit might have gone—Redfern's room at the hotel. And Benoit was unarmed and virtually defenseless.

If Cannon's guesses about Redfern had been correct, Benoit was now in grave danger. He began to run.

He burst into the hotel lobby. He took time for a hasty glance inside the hotel dining room. Then he took the stairs two at a time with scarcely a glance for Eve Redfern, who rose from the settee in the lobby and stared at him with startled fright.

He judged that Benoit could not be more than five minutes ahead of him, but a lot could happen to a man in five minutes. Five minutes was long enough for a man to die. Redfern, with his back to the wall, would be no more squeamish tonight than he had been the night of Martha Cannon's death.

Cannon ran along the hall and, without knocking, burst into Redfern's room.

Benoit lay on the floor, crumpled in a wholly lifeless position, and from a nasty gash on his head blood had oozed onto the worn red carpet. Redfern, gun in hand, stood over him, his eyes holding a crazy, trapped fury.

Immediately as Cannon burst in, Redfern's gun swung to cover him. Some of the trapped look faded from his eyes, and his lips split into a wolfish grin. "Well! Now I've got the two of you. And that's all I need, you realize that, don't you? Because Flora will go right on keeping her mouth shut just as she's been doing for years."

Cannon was inwardly cursing himself for his stupidity in entering Redfern's room with his gun holstered. He ought to have known better.

Redfern, his gun unwaveringly on Cannon's middle, said suddenly, sharply: "Turn around! Fast, damn you!"

Cannon hesitated. He saw the tendons in Redfern's hand tighten. His shoulders lifted in a helpless gesture of defeat, and he turned slowly.

His body was tense, and suddenly his back began to ache in expectancy of Redfern's bullet striking it.

Redfern said harshly: "Walk over to the wall. Raise your hands and clasp them behind your head. Quick! Move damn you!"

Cannon did. He knew he was closer to death right now than he had ever been in his life.

He debated making his try now, for he had no assurance that Redfern would not simply shoot him down in cold blood. With Redfern's position and wealth, the man could probably cook up some story that would be accepted. Redfern could claim that Cannon had killed Benoit, and that he had shot him in the back as he was leaving.

Cannon's muscles tightened. He would have thrown himself aside, but, before he could, the door burst open and Eve stood framed in the doorway. "Father! What's the matter? What's going on here?"

There was the smallest instant while Redfern groped for explanation while his attention was wholly diverted from Cannon. In that instant, Cannon acted. He whirled and drove across the room.

No time to draw his gun. No time for anything but hurling himself at Redfern's legs.

The gun muzzle dropped. The gun roared out in the closed, confined space. And then Cannon's body struck Redfern's legs and both went down in a tangle of wildly thrashing arms and legs.

He had Redfern's gun wrist in an iron grasp, and twisted viciously until Redfern gasped with pain and released the gun. Cannon snatched it up and came to his feet. He said breathlessly: "Eve, sit down. This is a long story and it's not very pretty. It started a long time ago, the day you were born."

He halted long enough to catch his breath. Redfern sat on the floor, looking up at him as though stunned.

Cannon went on: "Missus Redfern and Missus Benoit had baby girls on the same day. My mother was out at Singletree, helping. But due to a fall downstairs, Missus Redfern's baby died. Redfern persuaded my mother to help him exchange the children. You were taken from your own mother and given to Missus Redfern, who never knew you were not her own. You know what happened. Missus Benoit killed herself and Benoit left Singletree and took to living like a hermit. But as time went on, my mother's guilt became too much for her to bear. She told Redfern she was going to confess. He couldn't afford that. So he killed her. Flora Curtice saw him come out of our house that night. She saw him carry my father inside, unconscious. Redfern has been paying for her silence all these years."

He looked at Eve. Her eyes were wide, unbelieving. She said: "You're lying. It isn't so."

He stared at her steadily. She must have seen from his expression that he believed what he said, for a certain fearful doubt entered her eyes.

He said: "I've got Redfern's gun. I'm going to get the sheriff and Flora Curtice. I'm going to have Pa out of jail and Redfern in it before the night's over."

He took the key from the inside of the door and stepped into the hall. He closed the door behind him, locked it, and pocketed the key. He knew he couldn't trust Eve to go for the sheriff. In her confused state, she would naturally believe Redfern innocent. Instead of going for Kearns, she'd pick up the first member of the Singletree crew she saw.

He ran down the hall and took the stairs two at a time. He crossed the lobby, ignoring the curious crowd, and ran into the street.

The sun was setting now. Cannon ran toward the sheriff's office, Redfern's gun still in his hand, forgotten. Lord! He'd been so wrong all these years. He'd been so terribly wrong.

Behind him, he heard a window come up, heard Redfern's shout: "Turk! O'Dell! Dutch!" For an instant concern touched him, but it immediately went away. Redfern

90

was hooked. He'd never talk himself out of this one. And he wasn't, Cannon thought, the kind who'd try to fight his way out of it.

He met Kearns coming out of the sheriff's office. Quickly, before Kearns could see it, he stuffed Redfern's gun into his belt. He stopped the sheriff and launched into his story breathlessly.

Kearns listened with irritated incredulity. But as the story progressed, doubt entered his tired old eyes.

At last he said: "You say Redfern killed Benoit?"

Cannon nodded.

Kearns showed instant concern. He said: "And Redfern was yelling for Turk and O'Dell when you left?"

Again Cannon nodded, at last seeing what Kearns was getting at. Kearns broke away from him and began to run. "Then we'd better get over to Flora's place and darn' quick. Because she's the only witness left against Redfern."

Cannon caught up with him before he reached Main. Together, then, they ran toward the hotel. Cannon noticed that the upstairs window from which Redfern had yelled was now empty.

As they rounded the corner and headed for Flora Curtice's house, Cannon began to pull ahead. Suddenly, from behind Flora's backyard fence, a gun roared, and a puff of smoke revealed its position.

Kearns yelled: "Down! For Judas's sake, get down! They'll get you before you go fifty feet!"

Another gun puffed, and a fraction of a second later its report reached Cannon's ears.

But now his gun was in his hand. He swerved sharply, and headed directly for the fence. The two men who had been behind it now got to their feet, sure of him, sure they could cut him down before he could reach the fence.

Redfern. Where was Redfern? Cannon felt a touch of cold fear. Because he knew that Redfern had left these two outside while he went in. Even now Flora might be dead.

Kearns must have had the same thought, for he paid no attention to the pair behind the fence, Turk and O'Dell. Cannon triggered a shot at Turk, deeming him the more dangerous of the two, but it missed.

A bullet tugged at his sleeve, and a second took his left leg out from under him. He sprawled in the dust, sliding, holding his gun high so that the muzzle would not fill with dirt.

He saw the smoke billow out from O'Dell's gun muzzle, and stiffened against the bullet, which showered his face with blinding dust and dirt.

Then the two were vaulting over the fence, their faces grinning in sudden triumph.

Cannon rolled and thumbed back the hammer of his gun. Snap shooting, he fired at O'Dell and saw the man halt, saw a dazed, shocked expression touch his heavy face, then saw him crumple slowly into the street.

A bullet from Turk's gun plucked the gun from Cannon's fist and left his hand bloody and numb. Still lying in the dust, he rolled and, with his left hand, snatched Redfern's gun from his belt.

Turk, shooting from eye level now, carefully aiming, thumbed back the hammer for the final shot that would smash through Cannon's head. And Cannon, in desperation, snap shot at Turk as he had at O'Dell.

For a moment, he thought he had missed. Then, as he waited for the impact of Turk's bullet, the man's gun hand began slowly to drop. Turk's gun clattered to the street and he began to fold.

Before he hit the street, Cannon was crawling toward the

house. Redfern. There was still Redfern.

Shots echoed like firecrackers from inside the house. The back door opened and Flora ran out, screaming. She crossed the back yard and disappeared into the rear door of the hotel, directly across the alley.

Somewhere behind him, Cannon could hear another woman screaming. She seemed to be crying a name, a name that sounded like "Stuart!"

Consciousness began to slip from Cannon. He saw the tall, old form of the sheriff come from Flora's back door, smoking gun in hand. And then there was a flurry beside him and Eve was down on her knees in the street, lifting his head to her lap.

She kept saying, over and over: "Where are you hurt? Where does it hurt?"

Cannon grinned, feeling good for the first time in years. Hatred and bitterness had dropped from him like a cloak. He looked beyond Eve and saw Benoit staggering toward him, holding a bloody rag against his cut scalp.

Eve turned and followed his glance, and smiled uncertainly. "No. He wasn't dead. He was only knocked out. But Fath . . . Redfern didn't know that."

Cannon's grin softened into a smile. Because the hard, bitter, hating years were past. The ones ahead would be good, good for himself and Eve. And best of all, good for Lloyd Cannon.

He looked up into Eve's face, into her tear-bright eyes. What he saw there must have satisfied him, for he finally relaxed and let the pain and shock of his wounds claim him. All he needed now was rest and a quick recovery, so that at last he could begin to live.

Wild Waymire

I

Bleak and empty the land stretched, mile after mile of it. At times, it was almost level, until it brought up sharply against the foot of some rocky escarpment. From there, perhaps, it would become a bad lands of strange, eroded rock formations that reached away for miles before leveling again.

Grass grew sparsely, in scattered bunches and clumps. Sometimes a single plant would put up but a single blade. Yet this was the sustenance for thousands of cattle. Waymire cattle—Wheel cattle.

After years of breeding here, the cattle had grown used to the blistering heat of summer, to the cold, raw wind of winter. They had learned that the snow scoured first from the ridge tops, so it was on the ridge tops that they fed when the snow was deep. They had learned where the water was in the dryness of late summer, and would walk miles at day's end to suck from some tepid, moss-grown pool.

Harsh was the land, yet in its own way beautiful. Harsh was old Matthew Waymire, and his harshness had in no way been tempered by the beauty of the land. He could see none of it. He gave no notice to the flame of setting sun against a red sandstone cliff, or to the lace tracery of moonlight sifting through the naked branches of a cottonwood. A clear stream winding limpidly through the newly green growth of willows that bordered it was just a place to water a thirsty horse.

The dusty, hot cauldron of desert was a thing to be endured, the cool fragrance of shade at evening a thing to be sought for relief, but not enjoyed. The wild profusion of desert flowers in spring was only an irritation to Matthew, because some of them could poison his stock.

A sour man was Matthew Waymire, a bitter man. A man who lived with some cancer of guilt within in his mind. He read often from his huge, brass-bound Bible, yet unto himself he applied none of its gentler passages, only those which were harsh and unbending.

To Matthew Waymire, hating beauty, a woman's body was a sinful thing because it stirred his primal hungers and made them harder to control. Liquor was equally sinful, for it loosened the iron grip a man must always keep upon himself.

Guilt had damned Matthew to a lifetime of remorse. But the years had given him two hatreds to compensate for the misery of remorse. He hated Olaf Hunnicutt and he hated women.

Ernie Waymire, his older son, had been known to remark in moments of bitter rebellion: "I can understand how he might have strayed long enough to sire me. But Al puzzles me. Al's a year younger. Al proves that he must have done it twice."

Work and austerity were the order of the day at the Wheel. But the country said from the time the two boys began to mature: "He'll hold them down until something breaks. Five will get you ten that it ain't old Matt that breaks, either."

In the first, cool dusk of a summer night, Ernie Waymire stepped casually out of the house at the Wheel. He loitered for a few moments, making sure that old Matthew would not follow him out. He squatted against one of the peeled poles that supported the portico and shaped a cigarette. Touching fire to its end, he stared out across the bare and windswept yard.

The Wheel was strictly a working outfit. There was no grass here, save for that which grew of itself, no flowers or shrubbery. The ranch house, bunkhouse, and barn were all built low, of adobe bricks, and each had its long, pole-supported portico on one side. Cottonwoods, ancient and tall, sheltered the yard from the glare of sun at midday.

Hot, animal odors of barn and corral were heavy in the air, mingling with the pungent, spicy smell of sagebrush broken off by the horse herd as it was turned out at nightfall.

Suddenly, nervously, purposefully Ernie got to his feet and with swift strides put the yard between himself and the house.

He was tall, but there was no lankiness about him. His shoulders were wide and solid, and muscles rippled beneath his thin blue shirt as he tossed saddle up on the back of the gleaming sorrel he would ride tonight. Ernie's belly was flat, his thighs lean and long. His hands were large and broad. He wore a pair of gray woolen pants tucked into the tops of knee-high boots. Spurs made a pleasant *jangle* as he swung up into saddle.

Beneath his cowman's high-crowned hat, his face was somber and still as he stared back at the house. High cheek bones, faintly hollowed cheeks, and bright dark eyes gave him a look of fierceness, almost like that of an Indian.

It was plain that his thoughts were troubled. What he would do tonight, what he had done so many nights before, amounted to open rebellion. And he was too used to knuckling under before old Matthew's whims and prejudices for it not to bother him.

From the open door of the bunkhouse came the low, throbbing strains of some Spanish air, played on a guitar.

The liquid, soft voice of Ramón Ortiz sang the words meaningfully.

Suddenly Ernie grinned. A Spanish love song. Old Matthew would be loving this. He'd be sitting in the house, fuming, scowling, itching to go to the door and roar his order to Ortiz to shut up. But he wouldn't do it. He'd lost a couple of crews trying to ram his Spanish bit into their mouths. Good sense would keep him from trying it again.

Oddly stirred by the music, Ernie reined around and put his horse away from the corral and down the cutbank into the dry bed of Gila Creek. Climbing out on the other side, he touched his spurs lightly to the sorrel's sides.

Unlike old Matthew, Ernie was sensitive to the beauty of this open and empty land. Moonlight, blue-white, bathed the broad reaches of desert, washed the rocky escarpments in the distance with its glow. He began to think of Irene Hunnicutt, and the blood in his veins throbbed hot and fast. He let the horse run, enjoying this, the moonlight upon the land, the memory of music, the horse's power beneath him, and the anticipation of Irene's warm lips, her soft, white arms.

The Hunnicutts, father, two sons, and Irene, had a small ranch in a deep cañon some fifteen miles from the Wheel. There was bad blood between them and old Matthew, bad blood that had existed even before Matt and Olaf Hunnicutt had come to this hot country to settle. Neither Ernie nor his brother Al knew what the enmity was about. But they knew how real it was.

Olaf Hunnicutt was a huge, lusty, red-faced bull of a man. If Ernie had hunted through all of New Mexico for Matthew's exact opposite, he could have done no better than Olaf Hunnicutt. They were opposite in looks, in temperament, in outlook. Matthew was rich, Olaf poor; Matthew lived like a monk, Olaf for the satiation of his body hungers.

Ernie frowned, and slowed the sorrel to a pace that he could maintain over the entire distance. At ten, he sighted the cañon ahead of him, but instead of dropping into it by the road, he kept right, rising, and at last could look down upon the Hunnicutt Ranch from the high, cedared rim.

Tension came to him now. Moonlight, sifting through the jungle of ancient cedars, dappled the ground. Ernie threaded his way silently and carefully along the rim. Excitement kept rising in him, mingling with the tension in a way he found oddly pleasant.

He seldom considered nowadays what would happen to him if one of the Hunnicutt men found Irene in his arms. Nor did he think of the violence that would shake old Matthew if he knew. He was in the grip of something stronger than himself, stronger than any parental discipline.

He dismounted at the usual place, tied his horse, and advanced quietly afoot. His hands began to tremble slightly. Then he heard her voice, eager, soft, inviting: "Ernie?"

She came out of the moon-dappled darkness, straight into his arms. Her lips were scalding against his, her body firmly molded to him. There was a certain wild abandon about her that Ernie loved. The urge that gripped him when he held her was as elemental as birth and death, a thing that could not be denied.

Laughing shakily, she broke away, taking his hand. She was tall, only a head shorter than Ernie himself. Tall and strong-bodied, yet having a willowy grace that was all her own. She led him to where her horse was tied, to where a blanket was spread on the ground. She sat down, pulling him with her. Trembling, she pulled his face against her breasts. Soft they were, rising and falling with her agitated breathing.

Ernie raised his head. Moonlight fell upon the thin fabric of her dress, by shadow and highlight revealing each luscious curve of her body. He touched his lips to hers. She flung herself tightly against him. Her breath came raggedly.

Ernie pushed her away. His voice was hoarse. He said: "To hell with the Wheel. To hell with everything! I can't stand much more of this. I want you to marry me."

With unsteady hands he shaped a cigarette. She watched his face in the glow of the match, her eyes large and unreadable. When she spoke, it was as though something were forcing the words from her.

"No, Ernie. Not unless you will take me home with you to the Wheel."

"I can't do that. Damn it, you know why I can't."

"Because you're afraid?"

Ernie could feel a kind of cold fury stirring in his heart. He told himself that Irene did not really love him. He told himself that she was calculating and cold, that all she wanted was a place for herself at the Wheel. Suddenly he wanted to strike her, to hurt her. But he knew he would not.

He forced his voice to be patient. "I can't take you to the Wheel, and you know why. I've lived with Matthew all my life. There are just two things he hates . . . women and Hunnicutts. And you're both. You think you know Matthew, but you don't. If I took you there and told him you were my wife, he'd use names on you that I wouldn't use on a bitch dog. Then he'd run us both off. Is that what you want?"

She shook her head. "No. But I don't believe he's that hard. Once the thing was done, I think he'd accept it."

Ernie laughed harshly. "He's never accepted anything in

his life but his own way. I'll marry you tonight, tomorrow, any day you say. But we'll have to go away."

He wished he could see her face, wished he could see the play of expression upon it. But a shadow lay over it, hiding its expression.

She was silent, and Ernie's anger grew. He stood up, asking: "Are you going to marry me, or the Wheel? Do you want a husband or a ranch?"

"Maybe I don't want either one." There was a definite asperity in her voice. "I don't care if you marry me or not!" Her tone had risen sharply, but suddenly it softened. "Ernie, Ernie, don't quarrel with me."

"I'm not quarreling." This was not the first time he had asked her to marry him, nor was it the first time she had refused because he wouldn't take her home to the Wheel.

He made an impatient gesture with his big, broad hands, then stopped and raised her to her feet. He didn't particularly want to kiss her. But he did. He found her lips cold and unresponsive.

Anger stirred in him again. He said: "Are you afraid I couldn't provide for you?" Unreasoning was the desire to hurt her. "Or do you just want to get your hooks into the cash box at the Wheel?"

Even in the moon glow he could see her face go pale. He expected her to slap him for that. He saw two tears spill out of her eyes and run across her cheeks.

He said: "Oh, hell! You know I didn't mean that."

"No." Her voice was a whisper. "I know you didn't."

"What is it, then? What's the matter with you?"

She was crying openly now. Sobs shook her shoulders. She was silent for so long that he thought she was not going to answer. He longed to take her in his arms. He longed to agree to her demand. But he knew he couldn't. He knew how violent and vicious old Matthew could be, and Irene did not.

Finally she said, her voice so quiet it sounded forced: "I want to be proud of you, and I want you to be proud of me. I don't want to marry you and then slip away somewhere as though we both had guilty consciences."

Ernie waited for her to look up, but she did not. He had a quick and sure knowledge that she was lying, but he could not have said how he knew. It was a feeling that came to him, perhaps because they were so close.

There was a long, strained silence. Once she moved, as though to come closer to him, but instead she stepped away. Her rigid control of herself puzzled him.

Ernie shrugged. He said: "I'm sorry. It's just no good to-night, is it?"

She shook her head. "When will I see you again?"

Ernie said: "I don't know."

She would not let it go at that. With a kind of desperate urgency, she asked: "Saturday?"

"All right."

An unaccustomed obstinacy prevented him from taking her in his arms. He stared at her, seeing the pale, beautiful oval of her face, the silky sheen of her jet hair. Her gray eyes were pools of shadow. She turned away from him abruptly, picked up the blanket, and folded it. She tied it on behind her saddle, then untied the reins, and swung up easily into her side-saddle. Without a word or a backward glance she rode away.

Ernie stood for a moment, looking after her. Somewhere behind him, the dry limb of a cedar cracked.

He jumped, as though it had been a gunshot. He whirled, thinking even as he did: *A deer*. He shrugged, and began to shape another cigarette. He told himself, still thinking of that unexpected noise: *If anyone had seen us, they'd waste no time letting us know about it.*

But the self-assurance failed to quiet his chill feeling of unease. When he walked to where he had tied his horse, the location of that sharp sound lingered in his mind. As suddenly as he had heard the first noise, he heard a second—a crashing of brush, farther away, in the direction of the Wheel.

He swung quickly to his saddle, but realized at once that it was useless to try and give chase. The cedars stretched away for a couple of miles before they gave away to open desert.

So he turned and pointed his horse roughly in the direction from which the first sound had come. He kept his eyes fixed on the soft ground. After five minutes of circling, he picked up a track. Not a deer track. A man track with high heel and spur making their deep indentation.

Ernie Waymire felt a chill run down his spine. His stomach felt empty. His hands shook as he dismounted. He struck a match and stared down at the fresh track.

When he got to his feet, a sense of impending doom was heavy in his thoughts. Leading his horse, he followed the hoof tracks, finding a little farther on the branch that had been broken off.

He followed afoot until he came to the place where the man had mounted. Here, Ernie mounted, too, and set out following the tracks. It was slow going. Moonlight was bright, but not bright enough for trailing, and at last Ernie gave it up.

But he had established one thing. Whoever had watched them tonight had not headed for Hunnicutt's. He had headed for the Wheel.

II

Irene Hunnicutt rode slowly until she was out of earshot of Ernie. Then she rammed viciously with her spurs into her horse's side. Alternately her face flamed and paled. Alternately her body turned hot and cold.

Anger raged in her, and frustration, and shame. She knew a wild despair, for she knew that now Olaf would wait no longer.

She came into the yard just before midnight. A single lamp burned in the house. She supposed her brothers were both in bed. But Olaf was not. He was waiting up.

Fear touched her as she walked toward the house, but she made her face defiant as she went inside. Olaf looked up from his chair and saw the defiance immediately. She could not tell whether he saw the fear or not. He had been drinking.

He was a big man, a huge hulk of a man. Fat had begun to overlay his considerable muscular structure. Yet even without the fat he would have weighed well over 200 pounds. His face was ruddy, his eyes blue beneath the folds of fat around them. His mouth was generous, but now it drew into a thin line.

He said: "So you flubbed it. You can't make a go of it."

"I can. He'd marry me in a minute, but he won't take me home to the Wheel."

Olaf Hunnicutt laughed, but there was no humor in the laugh. Only a sort of unfeeling savagery.

"That's what he thinks! All right. You've had your chance to marry the Wheel. You couldn't make it. Now you'll marry Ernie. And I'll see that he takes you home to the Wheel if I have to go along myself."

Before, Irene's fear had been intangible, a vague feeling

that would not go away. Now, suddenly, it became very real. It was as though she could see the violence that would come from Olaf's threatened action.

She cried: "No! Give me a little more time. He'll come around!"

She wondered whether Ernie ever would. She didn't really care, now. This had started as a grab for Wheel, for revenge against Matthew Waymire. But it had changed when she had fallen in love with Ernie Waymire. Then it had been too late to stop.

Too, there had been her awful fear of Olaf when he was balked and defeated. There had been too many times when she had felt the fury that frustration could stir in him. He was a little mad, she knew. He was perhaps not responsible when temper took the reins. But that would not help her if she got in his way.

He said harshly: "Time, hell! You've had all the time you're going to get." He got up, stood over her like a gigantic bear. His face was covered with soft, blond whiskers.

Suddenly Irene's shoulders sagged. She didn't want it this way. But she knew her father well enough to know that there was no way out now. Hatred for Matthew Waymire was an obsession with him. He had built this scheme only to hurt Matthew, well knowing Matthew's hatred both for Hunnicutts and women in general.

Olaf asked: "When you going to meet him again?"

Irene felt a moment's rebellion as she visualized what would happen Saturday night. She said: "What would you do if I ran away with him? What would you do if I refused to go through with it the way you want it?"

Olaf's eyes glittered. His huge hands closed on her shoulders, and the fingers bit in cruelly, bruising, crushing. She gasped with pain.

His eyes inches from hers, blazing bits of icy rage, he said: "Why, I'd hunt you down. I'd tell him what part you had in this. I'd tell him how we planned it all, just to get our hooks on the Wheel. I'd tell him how you repeated to me everything he said to you, and I'd tell him how you laughed as you told it."

Irene cried: "But I didn't! I didn't do that. The things he said to me are private." Suddenly her shoulders sagged. She knew she was lost. She had made too much a point of wanting Ernie to take her home to the Wheel. He would remember that.

Olaf said: "He'll believe me, not you."

There was a certain apparent rugged honesty in Olaf when he wanted it to be. And Irene knew he'd bring it off.

He asked her again: "When are you meeting him?"

Irene said wearily: "Saturday night." She was in this now, and there was no getting out. But perhaps, if she tried, she could minimize the violence. Perhaps she could win Matthew over. At least she could try. She would try hard.

Olaf grinned. He said: "By God, I'm going to enjoy this." He struck a pose, scowling in fatherly outrage. "How's this?"

Irene said: "Oh, stop it. You won't have to act." She turned away toward the door of her room.

Behind her, her father chuckled obscenely. He asked: "How is Ernie, anyway?"

Irene's face flamed. She knew what her father meant. But she said—"He's quite well."—and slammed the door. Olaf roared with laughter.

Irene felt cheap and soiled. She slipped out of her clothes into her long flannel nightgown, and lay down on the bed.

What would Ernie think of her? He wasn't a fool. Sooner

or later he would put together her refusal to marry him unless he took her to the Wheel, and her father's sudden appearance at the place where they met. When Olaf tried to force him to take her to the Wheel, he would know that the whole thing was a put-up job.

Irene admitted that she was in this fix because of her own immature stupidity and greed. At first she had been willing to go along with Olaf's plan, for she knew, if they succeeded, she would become mistress of the Wheel. All her friends had married settlers or small cowmen, but she had dreamed of something better for herself than a one-room, dirt-floored cabin. Her face flamed again. Olaf thought her romance with Ernie had developed further than it actually had.

What was wrong with a man who would urge his own daughter to trap a man into a marriage that meant nothing to him but revenge? She knew the answer to that immediately. The cancer of hatred in her father's brain was more important to him than his own flesh and blood, more important even than life itself. Revenge against Matthew Waymire was all that mattered to him.

But revenge for what? That was something Irene had never been able to find out. What she did know was that until she had become old enough, Olaf had been helpless to take action. He had lived here on the fringe of the Wheel, running his cattle, letting his hatred fester and spread.

But as Irene had begun to fill out, turn into a woman, an idea had been born in Olaf's mind. Perhaps it had been born that day over a year ago when he had caught Ernie Waymire staring at her on the street in Cedrino. Perhaps he'd seen in Ernie Waymire's interest a crack in old Matthew Waymire's armor.

Irene could remember his first, red-faced anger that

Ernie dared to look at her that way. Then a week's quiet thoughtfulness had followed the anger. At last had come laughter, and the plan.

She recalled his coarse words: *Old Matt'd step right over a woman. But his sons won't. By God, his sons won't.*

And Ernie hadn't. Irene felt hot as she remembered how easily she'd fanned his interest. It had been a game, and a chance at wealth and security. Then she had begun really to care for Ernie, and it hadn't been a game any more.

She began to cry—hot, bitter tears of self-reproach. Why couldn't she have seen then how wrong it was to trifle with love and marriage for material gain? Why couldn't she have seen before it was too late?

Now she was realizing that a man might grow to hate a woman he was forced to marry. And she was wishing she had accepted Ernie, had fled with him before Olaf got ready to force the issue.

She hid her face in the pillow so that Olaf would not hear her sobs. She even considered getting up now, going to Ernie.

But she discarded that almost at once. Olaf's anger, once aroused, was terrible and merciless. He could and would carry out the threat he had made. Irene shivered, frankly afraid.

At the Wheel, Matthew Waymire and his sons ate in the ranch house. Matthew did not follow this procedure out of consideration for the crew, but because he found their conversation distasteful. Sometimes their talk would concern itself with work, with the problems of the ranch. More often it would deal with the fleshpots of Cedrino, with the bizarre exploits of the men at Sadie McCarran's parlor house, with their wildly exaggerated luck at the poker tables in the back room of the Horsehead Saloon.

As Ernie came into the kitchen, the rising sun put its red glow on the sprawling adobe buildings of the Wheel headquarters. Like blood, it flowed in through the windows, lighting the walls inside. Ernie fixed his eyes on Matthew as his father said harshly:—"Where were you last night?"—and gave him a cold, unblinking stare.

Ernie had a brief moment of uncertainty, but quickly decided that, if Matthew knew, he would hardly be this calm. When the uncertainty passed, resentment came.

He said, sitting down, looking straight at Matthew: "Listen. I do my work around here. I'm not a kid any more. I'm twenty-five. What I do after I'm through working is my own damn' business."

It was the first time he had gone this far in asserting his independence. Always before he'd either made up some convenient lie, or had avoided a direct answer. But this morning, for some reason, he knew he was through with lying, through with evasion. He was a grown man. It was time he stood on his own two feet and lived the way he saw fit to live.

Perhaps the sleeplessness and worry of the previous night had something to do with his sudden rebellion. Perhaps the spark of rebellion was born of frustration because he kept failing with Irene.

Matthew's stern and narrow face turned red. He put his fists on the table before him. The cook paused behind him with a coffee pot, waiting to see what he would do.

Matthew was not as large a man as Ernie. But his body was hard and strong as rawhide. A quick pulse beat in the distended veins of his forehead. His face turned darker, until it was almost purple instead of red.

But his voice was quiet enough. Maybe it was too quiet.

He said: "Oh. It's your business, is it? You've got to where you can carouse around all night, and it's nobody's business but your own?"

"I wasn't carousing." Ernie regretted instantly the defensive position in which the denial placed him.

"Then what were you doing?" Matthew's voice rose imperceptibly. There seemed to be a new tightness to it, a new wildness. His eyes, gray-green and cold as ice, were narrowed dangerously. His lips were tight and uncompromising. The pulse in his forehead beat faster. He began to breathe hard. He said: "Out rolling on the ground with some floozy, I suppose?"

Quick anger beat through Ernie. He heard his brother Al clumping toward the kitchen. Al came in sleepily and groped his way to the back door. After a moment, Ernie could hear the *squeak* of the pump handle, the *splash* of water on the plank well cover.

He checked his voice until some of the anger was gone. Then he said: "When the time comes that my nights interfere with my days, then I'll agree that you have a voice in what I do." He stared across at old Matthew, meeting the old man's eyes unflinchingly. It wasn't easy.

Matthew yelled, half rising: "By God!"

But Ernie cut him short. All the years of being held down suddenly piled up, a mountain of suppressed resentment. He said, trying to be calm: "I'm not like you. I like a drink of liquor once in a while. I like to dance, and I like to play poker. I like women, and there's nothing wrong with that."

Al came in through the door, mopping at his face with a towel. He began to grin delightedly, but Ernie didn't see him.

Matthew came to his feet, shaking with rage. He

shouted: "Damn you, if I can't train your mother out of you, I'll beat her out of you!"

Ernie said, not caring now what he said: "What did she do to you? Did she quit you for some other man? If she did, I'll be damned if I blame her . . . not if you treated her the way you treat Al and me."

He hadn't known the old man could move so fast. Disregarding dishes, food, everything, Matthew came over the table. Ernie staggered back, hardly having time to get his feet under him, then Matthew's fist exploded against his jaw. Ernie tried to raise his guard. Matthew brought a left from somewhere close to the ground. It smashed Ernie's mouth against his teeth. He felt the warm, salt taste of blood.

His right started its arc toward old Matthew's pointed, lantern jaw. But it never arrived. Ernie dropped his hands as suddenly as he had raised them. He couldn't hit his own father, not even in self-defense.

Matthew's right came in again. It seemed to make a pulp of Ernie's nose. He ducked his head and wiped away the blood on his shoulder, still not raising his hands. Matthew gave him a stiff left into his right eye. Ernie staggered back, recovering with difficulty.

A haze of rage seemed to grow in front of his vision. His voice came out, choked with fury: "That's enough!"

"Enough? Enough?" Matthew laughed crazily. "I haven't started! I haven't even started!"

He smashed three successive, driving blows into Ernie's unprotected face. Ernie fought the murderous anger that swam before his eyes. He tried to recover, to put up some kind of resistance, but it was too late. Matthew brought a right up from close to his belly in a vicious uppercut.

It *cracked* with the sound of a whip on Ernie's jaw. Matthew laughed crazily, his cold eyes showing some strange, perverted pleasure. Ernie's eyes glazed. He staggered. He put his back against the wall and held it there, gasping, trying to remain on his feet.

Al yelled—"Hey . . . wait!"—and began to move.

But Matthew's fists came in, right and left. The right smashed Ernie's mouth again. The left caught the sharp angle of his jaw.

For one brief instant, bright, whirling lights danced before his eyes. He could feel the wall at his back, sliding, slipping away. He felt the floor against his rump, then the room went black.

It might have been a minute. It might have been ten. He heard a groan, and the light began to come back. He realized that the groan had come from his own battered and swollen mouth. One of his eyes was puffed up.

He looked around the room with the other, the good one. Al sat in a chair at the table, eating. The cook was eying Ernie uncertainly. Matthew was gone.

Ernie struggled to his feet, stood there swaying while the room reeled dizzily before his eyes. When it began to steady, he stepped to the table and slumped into a chair.

Al grinned at him cheerfully. He said: "You talk too damned much."

All the anger was burned out of Ernie. There was something maliciously friendly about Al. Ernie had to grin back at him, but the grin didn't last long. It hurt his battered mouth too much. He said, looking up at the cook: "How about some of that coffee now?"

Al was laughing softly. He said: "You're a fool. You could have whipped the socks off him."

The cook, Germanic and stolid, poured out the coffee.

He was as dour as old Matthew himself. His face never altered. Ernie raised the steaming cup to his lips, winced at the pain. But he took a deep gulp and immediately felt better.

He said with some wonder: "He enjoyed that, Al. He really got a kick out of whipping me."

All the humor went out of Al. Like a candle snuffed out. A strange look came into his eyes, a look of intense hatred. "I know he did. I was watching him." Then the hatred was gone and again Al was easily smiling. He said: "You ought to know by now that you can't defy him. And you can't bait him."

The rage came back to Ernie, lurid and terrifying. He said with complete conviction: "He'll never do that again. Because next time I won't stand and take it. I'll kill him."

"Then you'd better get the hell away from the Wheel."

Ernie took a long draft of steaming coffee. He began to consider what his life could be away from the Wheel and the sour ill-humor of old Matthew, away from his nagging dissatisfaction with everything Ernie did, away from his sanctimonious rantings.

And once he had broken with Matthew, once he was gone from the Wheel, he knew Irene would come around. She'd marry him.

He stood up. Going to the window, he saw old Matthew riding out of the yard at the head of half a dozen cowpunchers. He said: "Al, I believe I will. I believe I will leave."

He waited until his father was out of sight. Then he stepped into the yard. Al came out and worked the handle of the pump while Ernie bathed his bruised and swollen face in the icy, stinging water. After that, Ernie dried off and went into the house after a clean shirt. With it on, he jammed his hat down over his head and went out to the corral.

Someone had watched him and Irene Hunnicutt last night. In view of his decision to leave the Wheel, it didn't matter so much who it had been. But Ernie was curious. He had until dusk to get his things together and pull out, for he knew Matthew would be gone all day.

He'd ride over to the bluff overlooking Hunnicutt's, and pick up that track, see where it led. Maybe he'd find out who had made it. Of course, it could have been one of the hands at the Wheel. But if it had been, Matthew would have the whole story before night.

Ernie grinned uneasily. Matthew had gone loco this morning. But that was nothing compared to what he'd do if he knew about Irene. Ernie knew he would have to leave before his father found out. If he didn't, he'd have Matthew's blood on his hands!

III

As Ernie rode, the sun rose on the eastern horizon, immediately hot, but growing hotter as the moments passed. It seemed to wither the grass. It beat down against Ernie's shoulders and battered face.

The numbness had left the bruises, and the swelling had run its course. But still he was scarcely recognizable as Ernie Waymire. One of his eyes was swelled almost shut. A big blue bruise was a blotch on one cheek bone. His nose was bulbous and intensely sore. His lips were cracked and puffy.

He cursed bitterly, and a wry grin spread out over his

face, causing him to wince. He told himself: *You ought to have known better.*

But there came an end to knuckling under. A boy knuckled under because he was small, because his will and resistance were unformed. But as boy turned into man, revolt became inevitable.

It might have been different if Matthew had ever showed either of his sons any affection. But he hadn't. Ernie doubted if there was even a capacity in his father for love. He was amazed, as he had often been before, that he, and Al as well, hadn't turned out more like old Matthew. He thought: *Well, that's one thing to be thankful for.*

Ahead of him the desert fell away, mile after mile of shimmering heat. Mirages appeared and disappeared as he approached them. He passed a long line of stringy cattle, making their way toward the shade of rocky badlands, returning from water. The tongues of a couple of the calves were hanging out, and a light froth lay over their mouths.

So far, the summer had been drier than most. Already half the water holes on Wheel range had dried up. The remainder had dwindled until it was difficult for more than a dozen cattle to water at them at once. Ernie wished it would rain.

It was about eight when he commenced to climb toward the bluff that overlooked Hunnicutts'. In the daylight, this was a different place than it was at night. The ground was almost barren of grass or other vegetation. There were only the cedars, and the long, green-and-yellow lizards. There was the occasional sign of a coyote, the occasional track of a deer. Off to Ernie's right stretched a huge flat of gray-green sagebrush.

He found the trail he had been following long before he came to the place where he customarily met Irene. Turning, he took this trail. A vast impatience seemed to take hold of him, and his mind shuffled through the hands at the Wheel, trying to decide which of them might have been crafty and sly enough to follow him.

He considered again the possibility that whoever it was had ridden out with Matthew this morning and would tell him what he had seen before the day was gone. This firmed his decision to leave the Wheel today. As soon as he'd verified his suspicion that the trail led to the Wheel, he'd pack up and get out.

He laughed. *Pack what?* He had an old six-shooter, a converted percussion Navy Colt. He had a beat-up Winchester rifle and a few clothes, work clothes. Nothing else. Nothing else at all.

He looked at himself with some surprise. He looked at his scuffed boots. He looked at his hands, brown and strong, roughened with work and weather. Hell, he was a fool. Since he'd been fourteen, he'd been doing a man's work. Not for wages. For bread and beans. He hadn't over $10 he could call his own.

He'd worked like any cowpuncher on Wheel, harder than most, for in him the sense of responsibility, of belonging was intensified. But for every dollar he'd had to go to Matthew. He'd had to ask for it. And because Matthew gave out a lecture with every dollar, Ernie had got so he didn't ask often.

He was following the trail with only part of his mind. With the other part he was marveling at himself—at Al. Why had they stayed? Ernie grinned. They had stayed because until recently it had never occurred to either of them to leave.

The trail deviated from the straight line between Hunnicutts' and the Wheel. It veered off to the left half a dozen miles before it straightened, and again took the direct route toward the Wheel.

Ernie thought: *He was afraid I might overtake him. So he turned away from the trail.*

He understood now that this spy, whoever he had been, had followed him away from the Wheel last night. Deliberately.

At noon Ernie followed the trail right into the yard at the Wheel. Al was gone. Ernie went to his room and shoved his few clothes into a blanket and tied them up. He strapped on the Colt and belt and, carrying the Winchester and blanket-wrapped clothes, went down to his horse.

The sorrel was one other thing he owned. He tied his bundle on behind his saddle and swung up. He took a look around the yard. Suddenly an overwhelming sadness possessed him. The Wheel was a big outfit, and by leaving he was relinquishing his rights to it. But that was not what bothered him. The Wheel was the only home he had ever known. Here were all the memories he had.

His face somber, he reined around and took the road toward Cedrino. He wondered what he would do, where he would go. If he had any kind of an outfit, he could run wild horses over on the Colorado line. But he had no outfit.

He shrugged. He was a top cowhand. There were plenty of jobs. And he would have Irene. . . .

Al Waymire rode into the yard at the Wheel not ten minutes after Ernie had left. He could still see his brother, a speck on the horizon in the direction of Cedrino. Al thought of Irene Hunnicutt. His grin faded and his eyes began to glitter. He had to give his brother credit. He hadn't thought Ernie had it in him.

All morning, Al had trailed Ernie, watching him from a

distance. And now, squatting in the shade of the corral, the feeling that there was opportunity for himself in this began to grow in him.

Al was different from Ernie in one respect. He admitted his own overpowering hatred for his father. He admitted it, but he didn't know what he could do about it.

He began to think of the color of old Matthew's face this morning as he had fought with Ernie. He recalled that pulse that had beat so wildly in the distended veins of Matthew's forehead. He remembered something else, too, something Ernie hadn't seen because he had been unconscious. Matthew had tottered and almost fallen as he had turned away from Ernie to the door.

Al thought: *Saturday . . . he's meeting her again Saturday.*

In some respects, Al was like old Matthew. He was as hard as nails, a fact he kept well hidden beneath his easygoing, laughing exterior.

The triangle in front of the cook house banged, and Al got to his feet. Waves of heat shimmered up from the sun-baked ground. He took a place at the long table with those of the crew who had not ridden with Matthew this morning.

Ernie's planned meeting with Irene Hunnicutt kept bothering him, and he ate his dinner absently. Afterward, he hunkered down against the outside wall on the portico, and shaped a cigarette.

Suddenly something that had evaded him all morning became clear in his thoughts. Matthew had a bad heart or something. Too much excitement could cause him to have a stroke or kill him outright.

Al considered this for a while. The plan that formed almost of its own accord in his mind caused the color to recede from his face so sharply that Ramón Ortiz grinned at him and said: "Heat getting you, Al?"

Al shook his head and forced himself to grin. But he was thinking: *What if I told Matthew about Ernie and Irene? What if I took Matthew up on that rim Saturday night?*

It didn't take too much insight to know what would happen. Matthew would blow up like a charge of dynamite. Ernie, having already taken one vicious beating at Matthew's hands, would be in no mood to take another, especially in front of Irene Hunnicutt.

Al began to smile. He thought of the long years behind him, thought of all the abuse he had taken from Matthew. He thought of Matthew's penury, feeling the same resentment Ernie had felt because he worked here at the Wheel for nothing but bread and beans, and of Matthew's lecture every time he wanted a few dollars to go to town.

He considered what it might be like if he were master of the Wheel's huge domain.

There was only one thing about his plan that he didn't like. There was no way on earth of controlling it. It was like dynamite in the hands of a child. No one knew which way the force of the blast would turn. No one could accurately gauge the damage that would be done.

Al wanted to hurt Matthew. And he wanted the Wheel. Beyond that he didn't care. He was willing to share the Wheel with Ernie, having always got along all right with his brother. But he was aware that in Ernie's present mood, there was infinite danger in bringing him and Matthew together.

But at last he shrugged. Hell, it was too good a plan to discard because someone might get hurt. Whatever happened, Al himself would be guiltless, for he would take no part whatever. What happened would be between Matthew and Ernie.

He got up and walked across the scalding heat of the

yard to the corral. Saddling his horse, he swung up and rode out in the direction of Cedrino. He wanted a drink, maybe two, maybe more than that.

As he rode, he tried to rationalize the deep feeling of foreboding that clung to his thoughts, and failed. Perhaps, if he had known that he was not the only man with a plan for Saturday night, it would have been different. He would have known the reason for the foreboding, and would quickly have abandoned his plan. But he knew nothing of Olaf Hunnicutt's plan for trapping Ernie. So he went ahead, in his thoughts, grimly determined that this chance for which he had waited so long would not escape him. . . .

Cedrino lay like a sore on the bosom of the desert, ugly, dirty, hot, and almost treeless. In the exact center of town was the plaza, a block square. It was intended to be a park, but it was only a weed-grown lot, baked and blistering in the afternoon sun.

Dusty streets surrounded the plaza, and, facing it on all four sides, were the town's business establishments. One building only rose above the others—the adobe-walled mission with its adobe bell tower. In the center of the weed-grown park was a statue of some early day Spanish *conquistador,* and a sagging plank bandstand.

Facing north, on the south side of the plaza, were the saloons, perhaps a dozen in all, ranging from the Mescal, where a peon could buy a drink for a half dime, to the Horsehead, the best, where the floors were clean and whiskey good.

Before the Horsehead, Ernie Waymire racked his horse. He looped the reins over the hitch rail and stepped into the shade of the covered walk. A dusty white dog sat beside the door, idly scratching behind one ear with a listless hind leg. A Mexican sat on the walk with his back against the wall. His straw sombrero was tilted over his face and he was snoring lightly.

Sweat stained Ernie's shirt, beaded his forehead. He thumbed back his hat, then took it off, and ran a hand through his damp hair.

There was perhaps a sort of reaction in him from the fight with Matthew. He felt drained of strength, lost, cut loose from all things that were familiar. With a quick, resolute movement, he shouldered his way into the saloon. It was empty save for Rod Garcia, the barkeep, and Oliver Kirby, who stood negligently at the long bar and toyed with an empty shot glass.

Ernie went to the bar, conscious of his beat-up appearance. He grinned at Garcia and said: "Draw me a beer, Rod. It's hot."

Garcia was round and fat. He wore a long black mustache. When he grinned, he showed Ernie a mouthful of gold teeth. The teeth were a vanity with him, a measure of the success he had found in life. They were simply gold crowns over perfectly sound teeth, because Garcia thought they were pretty.

He drew a beer in a heavy mug, waited a moment, then scraped the foam off the top of the glass with a polished stick. He shoved it along the bar toward Ernie. He did not remark upon the condition of Ernie's face.

Ernie drank half the beer, then wiped his mouth with the back of his hand. He threw a glance at Kirby, found the man regarding him with a speculative smile.

Kirby was a small man, dressed in a cream-colored linen suit. He wore a black string tie at the collar of his pleated shirt. A wide-brimmed, cream-colored Stetson sat on the bar before him. His hair was thinning and gray, worn long on the back of his neck.

He was a lawyer, and his voice, when he spoke, was slurred and musical, betraying his Southern origin. "So it finally happened?"

"What happened?"

Ernie liked Kirby, but he had never fully trusted the man. Kirby handled old Matthew's legal matters, and Ernie had occasionally suspected that both his and Al's boyish escapades had found a way to Matthew through Kirby.

Kirby was looking at Ernie's hands. He said, smiling gently: "You showed remarkable restraint, I would say. You let him beat you that way and never even struck back."

Something wild glowed in Ernie's eyes. He knotted his fists. He said: "This time. He won't put his hands on me again. I've left the Wheel, Mister Kirby. Know where I can get a job?"

He was thinking of Irene, and becoming aware that he had absolutely nothing to offer her. Today was Friday, tomorrow Saturday. Before tomorrow night he had to have a job, a place to live, enough money to begin life with Irene. If she would have him now.

Kirby pulled at his lower lip, a nervous, thoughtful gesture. He picked up his hat and settled it on his head.

He said: "Come on over to the office, and let's talk about that. You sure you have to leave the Wheel?"

Ernie nodded. There was a certain unreality to the complete wildness of his feelings. He was remembering the solid *crack* of Matthew's fists as they crashed into his unprotected face. He was remembering the sadistic pleasure he had seen in Matthew's thin, tight features. He said: "If he ever tries that again, I'll kill him."

Kirby pursed his lips. "Harsh words that you don't

mean, Ernie. You'll get over it. Come on."

They came out into the blistering heat of the street. Ernie winced. The dog still sat by the door, and, as Ernie stepped out, he began to scratch again at his sore and flee-bitten ear. The Mexican still snored lightly against the wall.

Not speaking, the two walked along the shaded, brick-paved walk until they reached Kirby's office. Next to it was the sheriff's office, and beyond that the two-storied adobe hotel.

Kirby kicked open his office door and waited for Ernie to go inside. He found a box of cigars, black ones, and offered one. Ernie took it and lighted up.

Kirby took off his hat and coat and sat down at his roll-top desk.

Ernie was looking out across the plaza through the small window. He was thinking how damned empty Cedrino was in the early hours of afternoon. Later, things would pick up. The townspeople would parade around the plaza in the cool of evening, and the saloons would fill. Music would drift from their open doors, and liquid Spanish voices would be singing.

Kirby asked abruptly: "How much money you got?"

Ernie laughed. "Ten dollars."

"What was the fight about?"

Ernie said: "I was out late. He wanted to know where, and I told him it was none of his damned business."

"A woman?"

"Maybe."

Kirby chuckled. He said: "It had to come."

He got up and went over to his small iron safe. He swung open the door, and, when he straightened, he had a small canvas sack in his hand. He tossed it at Ernie, and

Ernie, with a movement that was automatic, caught it.

"What's this?"

"A couple of hundred. You've got to live."

"Whose is it?" The money was solution for Ernie's problems, but a nagging suspicion troubled him.

"Call it a payment on your back wages. You've been working on the Wheel for eleven years. At thirty a month, that's . . . let's see . . . close to four thousand. I'll bet you haven't drawn over a hundred or two in all that time." There was an enigmatic smile on Kirby's face, partly obscured by his flowing gray mustache.

Ernie shoved the sack across the desk. "I can hear him laughing if I tried to collect," he said.

"You're entitled to something. Take it. I'll see that Matthew agrees to it."

Ernie wavered. He said: "Well. . . ."

Kirby shoved the sack into his hands. It had a heavy, solid feel to it. A man was entitled to something, after eleven years.

Coming to his decision, Ernie shoved the small sack into his pocket and stood up. If it had been only himself, he would have clung stubbornly to his pride and refused. But there was Irene to think about, too.

He said: "All right. It will be a help, sure enough. But this is all. This is all I want."

Kirby shrugged, smiling. His eyes were genial, yet somehow hooded and careful, too. Ernie shook his hand, finding it small and delicately formed.

He said—"Thanks, Mister Kirby."—and went out the door.

IV

Ernie paused for a moment before the lawyer's office, getting used to the scalding heat after the cool of the dark office. He saw Al ride into town, saw him rack his sweated horse before the Horsehead. He half turned that way, then halted. Al entered the saloon without glancing toward him.

The $200 in gold was a solid and comforting weight in Ernie's pocket. But he wished he could quit feeling guilty about taking it. Hell, Matthew owed it to him. That and a lot more that he'd never see.

He became conscious suddenly that he was hungry. He squinted up at the sun, deciding that it must be about three. He'd had nothing but a couple of cups of coffee since supper last night. No wonder he was hungry.

There was only one place in Cedrino where he ever ate. A little restaurant a block off the plaza, run by Ramón Ortiz's sister Rosalia. He headed toward it.

Now the town was beginning to come to life. A woman came to the door of her adobe hut and dumped a bucket of slop into the street. A couple of dogs rose from the dust on the shady side of the hut and sniffed at it curiously. An old-ster, hobbling along on a cane, spoke to Ernie pleasantly in a cracked old voice: *"Buenas días, señor."*

"Buenas días."

Ernie reached the restaurant and went inside. Always, inside these thick-walled adobe buildings, it was cooler. The place was furnished with iron-legged chairs and tables. Each table had a bright cloth on it. Ernie pulled up a chair and sat down. He could smell the spicy enchiladas and tor-tillas, the chili.

Ernie had been raised in this country. He had acquired a

taste for hot Mexican food, even in hot weather. He yelled—"Hey, Rosalia!"—and a slight smile curved his mouth.

"Hey, yourself." Rosalia came out of the kitchen smiling, but her smile froze when she saw Ernie's face. "Ernie! What happened?"

"I spoke up when I should have shut up." Ernie grinned at her.

She was two or three inches shorter than Irene. Her hair was jet black, having almost a blue sheen to it, and was drawn into a demure bun on her white neck. Her eyes were large, filled now with sympathy. Her lips, not having much color, were soft and full.

She said: "Your father?"

Ernie nodded. Somehow, her sympathy embarrassed him. He said: "I'll recover, but not unless I get something to eat."

"What do you want?" She was like this, sensing his moods, fitting herself to them. "I've been cutting up part of a hindquarter of beef. I could fry you a nice sirloin steak."

"Fine. That sounds just right."

Rosalia half turned, then came around to face him again. Her expression held a certain angered outrage. She said: "He's got no right to do that to you."

"He won't do it again."

Fear leaped into her eyes for the briefest instant. Then it went away. She asked: "You've left?"

Ernie nodded. Rosalia hesitated a moment more. Then she turned, saying: "I'll get your steak. Then we can talk."

Ernie tugged his sack of tobacco from his pocket and shaped a cigarette. In a moment, he could hear the steak sizzling as she dropped it into a skillet and, after another, could smell its rich, tantalizing aroma. He was ravenous, all at once.

He smoked the cigarette, got up, and tossed the butt out the door. As he had returned to his table, Rosalia came in, carrying a plate with the steak on it, and a side dish of enchiladas.

Ernie said—"Looks good."—and began to eat. Rosalia pulled out a chair across from him and sat down. Ernie ate with a studied concentration, not talking, and Rosalia watched him. Her eyes scanned his face, almost caressingly, but she lowered them hastily when he looked up. He finished, pulled his coffee over in front of him, and began to build another smoke.

He smiled. "That's better."

"Did you get enough?"

Ernie nodded. A silence fell between them while he finished making the cigarette, while he puffed it alight.

Rosalia's hands twisted in her lap. "Do you want to tell me about it?"

Ernie grinned. "Why not?" He colored slightly, finally saying: "I've been seeing Irene Hunnicutt."

Rosalia's hands clenched tightly together, but her face was composed. "And Matthew found out?"

"No. He jumped me about being out late. He didn't know about Irene." He began to smile. "Good thing he didn't, I guess, judging from the fuss he kicked up just because I was out late and wouldn't tell him where." His face sobered. "He used his fists on me. Somehow, I couldn't fight back."

Rosalia's hand came across the table and touched one of his big, weathered ones. "Of course you couldn't. What are you going to do now?"

"Marry Irene. Get a job. Find a place to live."

He stared into his coffee. He did not see the spasm of pain that ran across Rosalia's face. When he did look up, she was as composed as ever.

She said, almost inaudibly: "I wish you luck."

"Thanks." He fished in his pocket for a coin and laid it on the table. He found his hat and crammed it down on his head, grinned, and chucked Rosalia under the chin. "You always make a man feel better. Whoever gets you will be lucky."

He went back out onto the blistering street. He was surprised to realize that a great deal of the depression had left him. He found himself looking forward to Saturday night with excitement.

He went along the walk to the plaza. The door of the sheriff's office was ajar. Nate Gunlock, the sheriff, recognized him and bellowed: "Ernie! Come here a minute!"

Ernie went back and pushed open the door. Gunlock stared at him, but did not show quite the degree of surprise Ernie might have expected. Gunlock was a big man, over six feet one. He was gaunt, but his bones were big, his whole frame big. His eyes were bright blue, surrounded by crow's feet of genial humor. His mouth was wide and straight.

He asked: "What'd you tie into?"

"Matthew."

"Whip him?"

"No. I didn't fight him."

Gunlock stared at him speculatively. "Now what?"

"I left the Wheel. I'm looking for a job."

Gunlock snorted. "You're a damned fool. The Wheel will be part yours someday. Don't let him drive you out."

Ernie felt a rising irritation. "How many times do you think a man ought to stand up and let someone pound on him? You think I haven't got a temper? If I stayed there and he tried that again, I think I'd kill him. Then where would I be?"

Gunlock scratched his thinning hair. "Maybe you're right." He stared at Ernie for a long time. "You're a good cowman. You want to go out to my place and look after things? Thirty a month and beans. It'd save me riding out there every couple of days, and things'd get taken care of better."

The sheriff had a small outfit out at the edge of the desert, at the foot of the Spanish Peaks, thirty miles away. For fifteen years he had been putting whatever he could save from his pay into cattle, and now he had around 100 head.

Ernie said, feeling a sudden lift and showing it: "All right. That sounds fine. But I thought you were going to retire this year."

Gunlock shrugged. His grin was shame-faced. "I guess I'm too lazy. I guess I'd rather pound a swivel chair than a saddle, after all."

A sudden idea occurred to Ernie. It would explain Gunlock's lack of surprise at seeing his bruised face. He said: "You've been talking to Oliver Kirby, haven't you?"

Gunlock colored faintly, but he nodded. He said quickly: "But it ain't altogether Kirby's idea. I been needing a man."

Ernie said: "All right. I need the job, too. Thanks. I'll go out there tomorrow." He turned toward the door, but hesitated then, turning back. "I'm going to get married," he said. "I'll have a wife with me out there."

"Rosalia?"

Ernie shook his head, faintly puzzled. *Why did Gunlock think it might have been Rosalia?*

He said: "Irene Hunnicutt."

131

Gunlock whistled. He said: "Boy, it's a good thing you did leave the Wheel. It's a good thing you did."

"That's what I figured," Ernie said dryly.

He thanked Gunlock again, and went outside. If he hadn't planned to meet Irene tomorrow, he would have ridden out to Gunlock's place this evening. But it was too far for him to make another ride back tomorrow, so after hesitating a moment more he went into the hotel and engaged a room.

He knew he should be elated at the way things had turned out. With scarcely any effort on his part, he had acquired a considerable sum of money and a good job. Perhaps it was the very ease with which both things had been accomplished that fostered the uneasiness in him. Frowning, he tramped down the dark, cool corridor toward his room.

To forestall any idea Matthew might get of going to Cedrino and hunting Ernie up before Saturday night, Al Waymire waited until after supper Saturday to mention the tryst Ernie had with Irene.

He felt like grinning, but he was nervous, too. To Matthew, finishing his coffee at the long, kitchen table, he said: "I found out something you ought to know."

Matthew looked up, frowning at Al's tone. "What's that?"

"It's about Ernie. I found out where he was the other night. I figured you'd want to know."

"Damn it, speak up! Where was he?"

"On the bluff above Hunnicutt's. He's been meeting Hunnicutt's girl, Irene."

Al could feel the sweat breaking out on his body as he watched his father's narrow face go white. Matthew's hand froze on the handle of his coffee cup. For what seemed an eternity he was utterly motionless. Then the color returned to his face, suffusing it. That fast and dangerous pulse began to beat in his forehead.

He said hoarsely: "How'd you find that out?"

"I followed him the other night."

Matthew was on his feet. He moved like a cat, swiftly, without waste motion. His chair overturned behind him. He grasped the front of Al's shirt and yanked his son's face close to his own. His eyes were chips of ice.

"Damn you, why didn't you tell me before?"

Al shrugged, trying to squirm free. "I was trying to figure out what was the right thing to do. Ernie's my brother."

It was a good explanation, one that Matthew could understand. But in spite of Matthew's towering rage, Al had a feeling that his father despised him for his betrayal of Ernie. With a violent, savage movement, Matthew shoved Al half across the room.

Matthew's hands were shaking violently. He staggered, recovered only by clutching the edge of the table. Al waited until he seemed to be in control of himself before he said: "He's going to meet her again tonight."

Matthew's face was distorted, a mask of hatred and rage. He held his voice to a low, intense monotone. "Saddle two horses."

"Horses?" Al pretended not to understand what Matthew had in mind.

Matthew started across the room toward him. Al thought—*He's crazy! My God, he's plain crazy!*—and backed away toward the door.

Matthew roared: "Damn you! Saddle a couple of horses! Can't you hear?"

"Sure. Sure. I'll get 'em."

Al scurried out of the door. His own hands were shaking, his own knees were wobbly. Sudden fear stirred in him, fear that turned his body cold and clammy. So much intensity in Matthew scared him. No man ought to hate that much.

Behind him, the house was utterly quiet. From the bunkhouse, Al could hear Ramón Ortiz idly plucking the strings of his guitar. Somewhere, out on the desert, a cow bawled.

Al roped a horse and saddled swiftly. He roped another, and was cinching down the saddle on this one when Matthew came stalking from the house.

Matthew had belted his old .44 around his waist. In his hand he carried a long, braided whip. His face was gray, his eyes as hard and merciless as polished bits of granite. He did not even look at Al. Nor did he speak.

He swung up into saddle and whirled his horse so sharply that the animal reared in fright. Matthew struck him between the ears with the loaded butt of the whip. As the horse came down, Matthew sank his spurs into the animal's sides. Al swung up. Matthew was already across the dry bed of Gila Creek by the time he had reined around.

Al spurred his horse to a dead run, but it was almost a mile before he caught up with his father. Matthew was trotting his horse now, sitting straight and ramrod-stiff in his saddle. Al pulled up beside and slightly behind him.

Al was uncomfortable. And he was beginning to wish he'd let things alone. He was afraid now of what was going to happen. Ernie would never let Matthew's whip touch him, or Irene, either.

He looked at Matthew, looked at the sides of Matthew's horse. Blood welled from the spur gashes in the animal's sides. And there was blood on Matthew's spurs.

Suddenly, more than anything else in the world, Al wanted to turn back. He had a sudden premonition of disaster. There would be more blood spilled tonight than what was on old Matthew's spurs. And Al would bear the burden of responsibility for it. On Al's shoulders would rest the blame. . . .

Dave and Frank Hunnicutt stood beside the big pole corral and watched Irene ride out. Dave was big and blond like his father. He stared at the slump in Irene's straight shoulders. He had not missed the dull hopelessness in her eyes. Beside him, his brother Frank laughed nastily, and started to speak.

Dave said shortly: "Shut up." He stared at Frank. Frank had the same dark good looks that Irene possessed. But Frank had the soul of a weasel.

Frank sneered: "You act like you didn't want to do this tonight."

"I don't. She's in love with Ernie. Maybe she wasn't at first, but she is now."

Frank laughed again. "She's like all the rest of us. She's in love with the idea of owning the Wheel."

"Matthew'll never let her on the place."

Frank's grin was sure and unpleasant. "If he don't, he'll wish he had. Because you and me and the old man are going along to see that he does let her come to the Wheel. If he gets killed in the ruckus, so much the better. Then there won't be any question about it."

Dave shrugged. In his mind he could see Irene's face as she had walked from the house tonight. He felt an overwhelming shame. She had a right to something better than this. She had a right to work things out in her own way with Ernie. But she wasn't going to get it.

Olaf had gone to Cedrino for a minister, and he ought to be back now. Dave shrugged, and turned toward the house.

He hoped that something would happen, that Olaf wouldn't get back in time. He had a feeling that, if he didn't, Irene might get her chance to work things out for herself.

But his hope was short-lived. He saw Olaf's towering shape in the saddle of one of two horses approaching from the direction of Cedrino. And he saw the dark-coated figure of the minister beside him.

Shrugging, Dave turned and walked back to the corral to saddle his horse.

V

Olaf Hunnicutt and his two sons mounted and rode past the house on their way out. The minister, a small, frail-looking man, smiled benignly at them from the doorway. But Dave Hunnicutt thought there was doubt and uncertainty in the little man's eyes.

He looked at his father, big, hulking, bearded, and roughly dressed. A Remington revolver protruded from the old man's belt. A rifle was in his saddle boot.

Frank rode behind the old man, smaller, darker. Frank was clean-shaven, but there was a blue shadow of stubble over his pointed jaw. His eyes were set close to his nose. They were dark eyes, full of wildness and recklessness. Frank's mouth was cruel and twisted into a perpetual sneer. At Frank's hips rode two guns, two lightly seated guns with the holsters tied down. Frank fancied himself a gunslinger.

Dave, in range clothes as were the others, wore a single gun in a holster on his left side, butt forward for the cross draw.

They rode in silence, except for an occasional chuckle from Frank. The moon came up as they threaded their careful way upward. Near nine o'clock, they topped the rim. Here, they dismounted at a grunted command from Olaf. When the horses were tied, Olaf drew his sons together with a gesture.

He said softly: "No damned noise now. I don't want this to turn into a gunfight. We'll come up between them and the rim. You two keep quiet. Let me do the talking."

Frank began to chuckle again. Olaf slapped him with the back of his hand. "Shut up. Quit thinking about what you might see. She's your sister, damn you."

Frank snarled something unintelligible, and the three moved like shadows through the tangle of cedars. After ten minutes of cautious progress, Dave could make out the dark shape of a horse ahead. He touched Olaf on the arm.

"There," he whispered, and pointed.

Olaf halted. Frank, behind Dave, ran into him and muttered a low curse. Dave stared at the horse. After a few minutes he made out the figure of Irene, standing beside it. She seemed nervous, moving about restlessly, fidgeting.

After a moment, she moved away through the dappled shadows, but came back almost at once. Once, as moonlight struck her face, it glistened against the tears in her eyes.

Frank stirred slightly, and she glanced toward the three. But it was obvious she did not see them, although she probably knew they were here by now.

Shame stirred in Dave because he was a part of this. But he knew that with him, or without him, it would be the same. This plan had been in Olaf's mind for a long time now. As easy to talk Olaf out of this as to talk the sun out of shining on the broad desert.

Olaf hunkered down carefully against the gnarled trunk of an ancient cedar. Dave, standing, idly began to peel ribbons of bark from the trunk and shred them in his hands.

Time dragged. Shadows moved slowly as the moon traveled across the sky. Frank began to fidget until Olaf's great hand closed on his leg. Twice more, Irene left her horse, walking away in the direction from which Ernie would come. But both times she returned. The second time she was quite plainly crying, and her sobs were clearly audible.

At last there came in the sound of a horse running. That stopped, and Irene got up and ran toward the place where it had stopped. Dave could hear the soft murmur of voices, Irene's, and then Ernie's.

Olaf stood up, muttering softly but viciously: "Damn her, if she warns him. . . ."

But apparently his threat had done its work. She returned, her arm through Ernie's.

They heard her cry with quick alarm: "Ernie! What's happened to you? Your face!"

"I had an argument with Matthew about whether I could come and go as I pleased. I lost the argument, but I left the Wheel." He took her in his arms. He seemed elated. He said: "Honey, we're all set. I've got a job running Gunlock's place. I've got enough money to get married and buy what we need for the house." He held her away at arm's length. "Get your horse. We're going to Cedrino to get married . . . tonight."

Olaf nudged Dave, touched Frank with his foot.

Dave whispered—"Wait a minute."—but he knew it would do no good. He could feel Olaf's anger rising, fanned by the awkward position Ernie had put him in by asking Irene to marry him.

Irene began to cry, softly at first, more audibly as her control slipped away.

Ernie asked worriedly: "What's the matter? Did I say

something wrong? I thought. . . ."

Olaf moved. He had a gun in his hand. He said: "Damn you, Waymire! I ought to kill you. Sneaking around with her behind my back."

Ernie whirled around. Irene caught his arm as it snaked toward his gun. Dave stepped out with Olaf and Frank. Of the three, only Dave had not bothered to draw his gun. Frank held both of his, steadily centered on Ernie's belly.

Ernie probably would not have drawn his gun at all, thought Dave. Now he couldn't. A spot of moonlight struck Olaf's face. Dave could see the wildness in his father's eyes, the gloating grin on his mouth. Irene was sobbing, and she kept crying:

"Don't fight them, Ernie! Don't fight them! They'll kill you."

Ernie thrust her away. "Would that be so bad?"

He might have said more. But he had no chance. From behind him came a crashing of brush, and Matthew's enraged roar: "By hell, I'll fix you all!"

A shot spat wickedly in the tangle of cedars from which the voice had come. Dave's hand snaked his gun out of its holster as he leaped aside. He found immediate cover behind the trunk of a cedar. Olaf stayed in the open.

Matthew came charging out of the darkness, his gun spitting orange flame as fast as he could trigger it. He was making an odd sound, half snarl, half roar. Dave felt his eyes widen with amazement. He held his gun but he did not fire it. Matthew made an elusive, half-seen target in the dappled darkness, but it would not be that way long. He was coming forward at a run.

Ernie pushed Irene away from him so violently that she fell to the ground. She crawled away until she was close against the gnarled and exposed roots of a cedar. Ernie moved to intercept Matthew.

Dave had not thought Olaf could move so fast. In half a dozen strides, he overtook Ernie. His gun raised, and chopped down on Ernie's head. Ernie went down like a felled pine, groaned, and lay still. Irene gave a sharp cry of pity.

Matthew was only thirty feet from Olaf now. And directly behind him came Al Waymire, holding a rifle at waist height.

Dave thought: *My God, they'll all get killed!* But still he did not raise his gun. Olaf had planned all this, out of greed, out of a vicious desire for revenge. Let him now reap the harvest of his greed.

Olaf seemed intent on doing just that. He leveled his gun at Matthew, and the *click* of the hammer coming back was loud and clearly audible. Matthew dived aside. Olaf's gun thundered, and flame spat three inches from its muzzle. Behind Matthew, Al stumbled. With a crash he went to the ground, but in a moment was up again.

But now he stopped running. He walked, and he walked unsteadily. Because of the dark, his face could not be seen.

Frank was firing both guns at the elusive, moving targets that were the Waymires. Matthew turned his gun toward Frank, and Frank, hit, howled: "Dave! Damn it, Dave, get in this."

Dave stepped out, stepped closer, and brought his gun up. He wanted no part of this. Olaf and Frank were getting just what they had bargained for. But family loyalty forced him whether he liked it or not. He just couldn't stand aside and see either Frank or Olaf cut down.

Suddenly came that odd, distinctive noise, that sound a bullet makes when it smacks solid flesh. Al went down as if he'd been clubbed.

Frank yelled triumphantly: "Got that one! I got Al!"

Matthew whirled. He ran a few steps back to where Al lay, looked down, then knelt, and touched his son. He seemed utterly oblivious of the guns spitting behind him.

Dave yelled: "Frank! Quit it! Al's hurt!"

The grim humor of that escaped him entirely. The cry came out of him automatically. It was an instinctive cry, dredged out of his boyhood in which the play stopped when someone got hurt. But this was not play. This was reality.

Matthew got up and turned around. For an instant he stood illuminated by moonlight, and his face was terrible to see. In the moon glow it was blue-gray. But the eyes were alive, blazing. Hot eyes. Eyes of a man who wanted to kill.

Frank was reloading one of his guns with fumbling, frantically anxious fingers. Olaf stared at Al, lying on the ground, then at Matthew.

He said: "Matt, is he dead?" He held his gun straight down at his side.

Matthew nodded. His voice had a terrible quality to it. It shook. He said: "Yes, he's dead." He swayed, as though a strong wind was blowing against him. A spasm of pain crossed his face. His gun dropped from his nerveless fingers. He toppled, and fell across Al's body.

Olaf breathed: "He was hit, after all. I didn't see how we could miss him as often as we shot at him."

Dave felt drained of feeling. His knees were trembling violently. He shoved his unfired gun back into his holster.

Frank said complainingly: "Dave didn't even shoot."

Olaf didn't seem to care. He stood hesitantly for a moment, plainly appalled at the damage that had been done, at the suddenness with which the violence had stopped. He pulled himself out of this with an effort. The shock wore off, the surprise. He began to laugh.

141

He turned and spoke to Dave: "You and Frank load Ernie on one of the horses. We're keeping that preacher waiting."

Dave walked away, filled with sudden disgust. Two men lay dead back there, another lay unconscious. Yet Olaf could laugh. His shouted laughter followed Dave as he walked swiftly through the cedars toward the rim. Dave shuddered. The insane roar of Olaf would not let him alone.

"The Wheel! It's ours! By the gods, boys, the Wheel is ours!"

Dave untied the horses and led them back. Irene still sat between two huge tangled roots of the cedar where she had fallen. She was not crying now. She was utterly silent.

Dave handed the reins to Frank and went over to her. He stooped, caught her beneath her arms, and raised her to her feet. Her eyes were wide with shock, her face deathly pale. Her voice was like that of a sleepwalker.

"Is he dead?"

"Ernie? Uhn-uh, honey. Ernie's all right. You're going to marry him tonight."

"He doesn't want me."

"Sure he does. I heard him ask you."

"That was before. . . ." A long shudder went through her.

Dave put his arm around her. He led her over to where her own horse was tied. Behind him, Olaf and Frank hoisted Ernie's limp body into the saddle of one of the horses.

Olaf said: "Dave, ride behind Irene. See she don't try nothing. We're using your horse for Ernie anyway."

Frank asked—"What about them?"—and gestured with his head at Matthew and Al.

"Leave 'em be. We'll come back after 'em when Ernie's one of the family."

Dave lifted Irene into her side-saddle and swung up behind her. The horse fidgeted, but Dave's iron hand held his head up. He reined around and started toward the trail. Behind him, he could hear Frank and Olaf, still tying Ernie's body down.

Sick with disgust, Dave rode on. Irene was trembling, as if she were cold. But her tears had stopped.

Dave was almost out of earshot when he heard Frank ask: "What'd you mean, the Wheel is ours? Ernie's still alive. You going to kill him, too?"

And he heard Olaf's laugh, the laugh he was growing to hate. "Hell, we don't have to kill him. He's a wanted man. You seen him kill Matthew, didn't you? He wouldn't let Matthew beat him no more, and he killed him."

So that was it? Marry Irene to Ernie, giving her a claim on the Wheel. Send Ernie to running, wanted for Matthew's murder. Then the whole Hunnicutt family could move in at the Wheel.

Dave had to admit that it was so simple it couldn't help but work. Al's death would also be laid to Ernie. Ernie wouldn't stand much chance if they caught him. He probably wouldn't even go to trial. This was wild country and folks would stand for a lot of things. But they wouldn't stand for a man's killing his own father and brother. They'd shove the sheriff aside and hang Ernie from the nearest cottonwood.

Fate had played perfectly into Olaf's hands tonight. He had planned a part of this, but the presence of Matthew and Al had been pure luck.

As he had wondered so many times before, Dave wondered again at what it was that had been between Matthew and Olaf, at what could have caused them to hate each other so violently.

He started down the trail, hearing the noise made by the other three horses behind him. He heard the racket of shots as Olaf emptied Ernie's gun into the ground. Below winked the light in the windows of the Hunnicutt ranch house.

Whatever the cause of the hatred that had festered so long in Olaf's mind, it was wiped out now. At the cost of Irene's happiness, and perhaps of her sanity. At the cost of Ernie's life with her. At the cost of Al Waymire's life, as well as Matthew's.

What should have stayed strictly between Matthew and Olaf had spread to encompass all of Olaf's family and all of Matthew's, as well. Nor was it through spreading.

Dave wished Irene would cry. She was like stone in the saddle before him now, stiff and cold and unmoving.

He said: "Honey, don't worry. It'll work out some way."

She shook her head slowly, dazedly. "He'll hate me. He'll blame me for Matthew's death and for Al's. He'll blame me."

Dave said: "No he won't."

But he knew he was lying. For every time Ernie entered a strange town furtively, he'd be blaming her. Every time he had to leave one hastily, he'd be blaming her. He'd blame her because he couldn't sleep soundly, and he'd hate her every time a Wanted dodger caught up with him. That would be natural and inevitable.

But there was no changing it. Even if he'd thought it would do any good, Dave knew he could never betray his own kin. He couldn't turn Olaf and Frank over to the law to save Ernie. So Ernie would have to run. It was the only way.

He rode directly to the house when they arrived. He

slipped to the ground and lifted Irene down. Her apathy scared him, as did the staring look in her eyes.

He said: "Go on in, honey. I'll be back as soon as I take care of your horse."

The minister came to the door. His smile was not so benign now. There was plain fright in his eyes. But he was gentle with Irene, perhaps sensing that she was as much a victim here as he was. Again, Dave felt the stir of shame.

He led Irene's horse across the yard to the corral, off saddled, and turned the horse in. Then he trudged back toward the house.

Olaf and Frank came into the yard off the trail, and Dave helped untie Ernie and lift him down. Ernie groaned and stirred, but he could not stand up. Olaf laughed and tossed him across one shoulder. He carried him into the house. Dave followed.

Olaf said: "Here's the groom. Throw some water in his face so's we can get on with it." To Frank, standing in the doorway, he said irritably: "Take care of the horses."

The minister looked at Ernie, slumped in the chair where Olaf had dumped him. His face was pale. He said: "I don't know . . . I don't think I will perform any ceremony here. There is something wrong."

Olaf grabbed his shoulder. Olaf's fingers bit deeply, and the minister winced with pain. Olaf said: "The hell you won't!"

He flung a dipper of water into Ernie's face. Ernie gasped, shook his head, and opened his eyes. Olaf went across the room and yanked Irene to her feet. He dragged her over to Ernie.

Then he said: "Get on with it. We ain't got all night."

VI

The minister hesitated, holding his heavy Bible. Olaf's face darkened. He put a hand on his gun. Irene took Ernie's hand hastily and drew him to his feet. Ernie was barely conscious, but he could stand.

Irene looked at the minister and said: "You had better do it. It's all right. I love the man you're to marry me to. I . . . I'll make him as good a wife as I can."

The minister seemed relieved. He opened his book. But he was still trembling, and his voice was not steady.

"Dearly beloved, we are gathered here in the sight of God to join this man and this woman in holy wedlock. . . ."

Irene could feel tears welling into her eyes. The words were beautiful.

"Do you, Irene, take this man to your lawful wedded husband, to love, honor, and obey in sickness and in health so long as you both shall live?"

"I do." Irene could not keep a sob out of her voice.

"Do you, Ernest, take this woman . . . to have and to hold, in sickness and in health, for better or for worse, so long as you both shall live?"

Ernie shook his head, as if to clear it. Olaf's gun prodded him viciously in the spine, and the *click* of the hammer going back seemed thunderous and ominous in the silent room.

Irene looked up. Ernie was scowling. A stubborn look was in his eyes. He was beginning to comprehend, through the dizziness and pain in his head, what they were doing to him. He could not know that Al and Matthew were dead. He looked down at Irene, his eyes blazing. He turned around and looked at Olaf. Olaf prodded again.

Irene stared at her father. She could see the wildness

growing there. Olaf's brain wasn't working now. Only his instinct and feelings. If Ernie refused, Olaf's bullet would tear through him.

Irene's hand tightened on Ernie's arm. She looked up at him. He might not heed her plea now, hating her, but she had to try. She had to try and save his life. She begged: "Please, Ernie! Please!"

He looked back at the minister. It took a moment for his face to settle, for the rage and hatred to go out of it. At last he said: "I do."

The rest of it was mercifully short. And at last the minister said: "I now pronounce you man and wife." He slammed his Bible shut and looked around frantically. He was like a rabbit, terrified, on the point of heedless flight.

Olaf's laugh boomed out. He roared: "Frank! Take the man back to town. Stop and see Nate Gunlock. Tell 'em what Ernie's done."

Ernie swung around. His mind was apparently getting clearer all the time. He said: "What have I done?"

"What've you done? Why, you damned fool, don't you remember? You killed Al, and then you killed Matthew. I slugged you, but I was too late to stop you."

Ernie's hand snaked his gun out of its holster. He backed toward the door. He said: "I don't know what's going on, but I haven't killed anybody."

Olaf laughed. "Go ahead. Run. It's all you can do now. Frank and Dave and me all saw you kill Matthew and Al both. Look at your gun. It's empty."

Ernie glanced down at his gun. A look of surprise came over his face. He felt for shells in his empty belt. Again, he shook his head. A hand went up to feel gingerly of the lump that Olaf's gun barrel had put on it.

Irene wanted to cry. Ernie looked at her. She had never

seen so much hatred in anyone. It seemed to wither her soul.

Ernie said, his voice bitter and harsh: "You're a part of it, too. It was all a rotten game, wasn't it? All you wanted was the Wheel." He shrugged, but the hatred in his eyes didn't lessen. "You've got it now. But I'll be back. I'll get things figured out, then I'll be back."

He backed through the door. Irene could hear the sounds that Frank made, leaving with the minister for Cedrino.

Olaf laughed again. He bellowed: "Let 'im go, Frank!"

Ernie ran halfway across the yard toward the corral, then slowed to a walk. Olaf went out to watch him. Irene and Dave followed. She wanted to call out, she wanted to run and catch up with Ernie, to beg, to plead, to make him believe her. She wanted to tell him how this had really happened.

Olaf called mockingly: "Take the best horse there, Ernie. You'll need him. Besides, nothing's too good for the ex-owner of the Wheel."

Irene thought for a moment that Ernie would come back. But he must have begun to perceive the enormity of the evidence that was stacked against him. He mounted and rode away without a backward glance.

Ernie's head felt as if it were an anvil on which a blacksmith was regularly beating with his hammer. It throbbed, and, each time it did, his vision blurred. Just beyond the yard he halted, overcome by nausea. He dismounted quickly and retched. Pale and sweating, he remounted and nudged the horse ahead.

It hurt him to think, but he had to. He had to figure out what was happening, and most of all he had to figure a way out of it.

Wild Waymire

It was a distinct shock to think of both Matthew and Al dead. He tried to supply the gaps in his memory. He'd ridden into the cedars to meet Irene. He'd met her and she'd been crying. He'd asked her to marry him.

It was coming back now, slowly and hazily. His memory had an aura of unreality to it. Olaf and Frank and Dave had jumped out of the darkness. He could remember Olaf's cursing him. Then he could recall gunshots, and Matthew's crazy, enraged voice. He'd started for Matthew. That was it. That was all he could remember.

In a half daze, he thought: *Maybe I did do it. Maybe I thought Matthew was going to work me over again. Maybe I did kill him.*

He became aware that his horse had halted, had dropped his head to graze. The horse was moving from one clump of grass to the next, tugging, yanking. It took half a dozen plants to make a mouthful. Ernie pulled the horse's head up, and touched his ribs with his spurs. The horse moved out briskly then, and Ernie kept him moving, kept his head up.

He had no idea at all where he was going. Desperately he forced his mind to work just a little longer. He decided that the only logical place to head for would be the Spanish Peaks at the edge of the desert. He'd stop and get some sleep and grub at Nate Gunlock's place. Nate would be scouring the desert for him. But he probably wouldn't look at his own ranch until it was too late.

With his destination decided, Ernie sagged in his saddle, half dozing. His chin dropped down onto his chest. He had a bad concussion, but he didn't know that. All he knew was that his head hurt terribly, that he was nauseated, and that he could hardly stay awake.

Even his horror at the predicament he was in seemed unreal to him now. Like a dream. Like an awful bad dream.

Dazed as he was, his mind would not let the problem alone. The hours passed, and horse and man crawled across the desert, bathed with the weird glow of moonlight. Riding became a nightmare for Ernie, a nightmare of tortured thoughts, of pounding pain in his head. With each step the horse took, the pain seemed to increase.

Dawn came, gray and cold. The eastern sky turned pink, and the sun poked its way above the broad, flat desert. The glare of the sun against the land brought new waves of dizzying pain to Ernie's head.

But at last he made it. At last he raised the log shack that was Gunlock's ranch house. He dismounted before the ramshackle log shelter that served as a barn, watered his horse in the creek beside it.

He lay down, belly flat on the ground and sucked up water himself while the horse drank. He sloshed the cool water over his head, into his face. He tried to wash away some of the clotted blood in his hair over the knot, but abandoned this because the spot was too sore.

When he rose, he led the horse into the barn. He clawed a feed of hay out of the loft for the animal and unsaddled him. Then, shutting the door, he made his way, staggering, toward the house.

He didn't even bother to remove his boots. He fell across the dusty, dirty bunk and immediately lost consciousness.

It was dark when he awoke. Fear clawed at him because he did not immediately place his surroundings. Moonlight shone in the door, laying a square of illumination on the dirt floor. Ernie's head felt light, but it no longer ached. Without moving, he stared around at the dimly lighted cabin.

It began to come back. Irene, Olaf and his sons, Matthew, and Al. The marriage ceremony. His flight. He sat up abruptly. He expected the pound of pain to recommence in his head, but it did not. He made a wry grin at that.

He realized now that he was ravenous. He wondered what time it was and wandered out through the door to look at the moon. It lay low on the western horizon.

Ernie grunted: "Be getting light soon."

He stared around. In far distance he heard the lonely howl of a wolf. The creek, narrow and small, made its cheerful, gurgling noise down by the barn. Behind the cabin, the Spanish Peaks loomed up, ghostly and unreal. Ernie's horse made small stirring sounds from the barn.

Ernie walked to the creek and got down to drink. The water was sweet and cold. He drank until he thought he would burst.

Returning to the cabin, he found a candle and lighted it. It occurred to him with a shock that he was a wanted man, that he was a fool to show a light here. The realization that he was wanted for the murder of his father and brother was a bitter pill to swallow. He blew out the candle, went to the door, and listened intently. He began to know the terror of a hunted animal.

A sudden, wild rage possessed him. Dark-eyed, hollow-checked, intent and bitter, he made a savage, lean shape in the doorway of the old cabin. With an impatient gesture, he stepped back and closed the door.

He went over and re-lighted the candle, then stared about with questing, hungry eyes. He found a box of .38-caliber cartridges that would fit the Colt conversion in a cupboard. Beside the cartridges were several cans of beans and a small sack of coffee. An empty bean can contained sugar, which was covered and protected by a piece of newspaper stuffed into it on top of the sugar.

In one corner of the room was a gunny sack. Ernie got it and stuffed the canned goods into it. The coffee and sugar followed. He found a can of lard and some flour and took that, too. Ernie missed his rifle, but there was no help for that. It was back at Hunnicutts' in his saddle boot.

Prodded by his uneasiness, he shouldered the sack and went outside. He saddled his horse, tied the sack on behind, and again watered the thirsty animal in the creek. Then he swung up into saddle and took the trail that headed up toward the Spanish Peaks behind the cabin.

He had a bleak vision of what lay ahead of him now. Running and more running. Nothing else. Every sheriff and town marshal would be his enemy. Sound sleep would become a thing unknown to him. He must live forever with his hand close to his gun.

He thought of the vast acres that comprised the Wheel, of the thousands of cattle that roamed this land and carried the Wheel brand on their hips. And he thought of the Hunnicutts and Irene, entrenched firmly in the Wheel ranch house.

He admitted at last that he was a fool. He should have blankly refused to marry Irene last night. He considered this for a moment, then shook his head. Irene had not been the only one to look into Olaf Hunnicutt's eyes last night. Irene had not been the only one to see the murder there. If Ernie had refused to marry her, he would not be here now. Olaf had planned too long. Pure animal rage at being frustrated would have tightened his finger on the trigger.

Ernie's mind was like a coyote in a cage, questing back and forth ceaselessly for an opening in the cage. But there was no opening. There was no hope that things could ever be different than they now were. And with this realization, Ernie Waymire knew sudden and complete despair.

VII

Standing in front of the house, Olaf watched Ernie ride away. He saw him pause at the edge of the yard, heard the sound of his retching. He grinned. Dave stood at his shoulder, frowning.

Olaf swung around and asked: "What was the matter with you up there? Scared you'd get hurt?"

Dave's frown deepened. "I didn't like what you were doing. I don't like it a damned bit better now."

"But you'll come along with the rest of us to the Wheel, won't you? You don't mind getting the benefit from what I'm doing." Olaf was mocking.

Dave shrugged. Irene had gone into the house. It was utterly silent in there.

Olaf said: "We ain't through yet. There's still two bodies to be fetched in." He moved away toward the corral.

Dave threw a glance at the house, then followed reluctantly. He took his rope off his saddle and went into the corral. Roping out a big gray, he slipped a bridle onto the animal, then led him out, and saddled up. He hung his rope back on the saddle.

Olaf roped out a bay mare, and, when he had saddled, the two rode out of the yard.

They took the trail that led up onto the rim, and twenty minutes later came out on top. They rode at once to where the bodies of the two Waymires lay. Dave stared down at them. He had known Al pretty well, and there had been a time when he'd liked him. He wondered why he should feel so guilty about this. He'd fired no shots himself. He'd taken no active part in what had happened. But the guilt remained. He couldn't rationalize it away.

Olaf grunted: "Hunt around and find their horses. They can't be too far away."

"All right."

Dave reined his horse around. He didn't feel any particular regret about Matthew Waymire. Matthew had been thoroughly disliked by everyone who had known him even slightly. So far as Dave knew, Matthew had had no redeeming traits at all. He had been hard as nails, cruel, narrow-minded, egotistical. He had been soured with hatred and with bitter memory. What memory? What had been between Olaf and Matthew?

His horse pricked his ears forward, turning his head to the right. Dave reined him that way, and a few minutes later heard a whinny from directly ahead of him.

He found Ernie's horse and later the other Waymire horses tied to the low branch of a cedar. One of them had a dozen raw open spur gashes on each of his sides. Blood had run from the open cuts and had dried, black and stiff, on the animal's belly.

Dave thought: *Matt was in a hurry all right.*

He dismounted and untied the horses' reins. Holding them, he remounted. He heard Olaf's great voice lift in the distance.

"Dave! Dave, come here, quick!"

Dave touched spurs to his horse's sides. The reins of the led horses tightened, almost dragging him from the saddle. Then the trailing horses jumped ahead, and the reins slackened.

At a canter, that was the fastest pace at which he could lead these horses without losing them, Dave made his way back to Olaf. His father was kneeling beside the body of Matthew Waymire. Olaf looked up. His face was pale. It was getting dark.

He said: "Matt ain't cold. Al is. Maybe Matt ain't dead."

Dave dropped the reins of the led horses and dismounted. He knelt beside Olaf, dropped his head to Matthew's chest, and listened. He heard the faint, irregular beat of Matthew's heart.

Olaf said: "Well?"

"He ain't even about to be dead." Dave couldn't help grinning at the shock in Olaf's face. He couldn't help feeling an obscure pleasure at Olaf's discomfiture. He asked: "What you going to do now?"

"Maybe he'll die. Where's he hit?"

Dave struck a match. He hunted over Matthew's chest and abdomen, but found no sign of blood. He turned Matt over and looked again. There was no wound. The match burned his fingers, and he flung it away. He lighted another and inspected Matthew's legs and arms.

He stepped on the match. "He ain't even hit."

Olaf's voice rose. It was almost a roar. "He's got to be hit! Damn it, a man don't just fall down and pass out. Not Matt's kind of a man anyway."

He pushed Dave away roughly. Dave was glad the darkness hid his grin. Olaf struck a match and looked for himself. When it burned down, he struck another. He used five matches before he was satisfied.

Dave asked: "Now what? You going to kill him?"

He didn't really believe that Olaf was that cold-blooded. He didn't believe Olaf could deliberately murder a man in cold blood.

Strangely Olaf was trembling. Dave could see the struggle he was having with himself. He could see Olaf's trying to adjust himself to this new complication.

Dave said: "Think about it later. Let's load 'em up and take 'em home."

"All right." Olaf seemed glad of the chance to postpone his decision. Dave led one of the Waymire horses over and they loaded Matt first. They loaded Al's body then, and tied it down. The horses didn't like the inert weight and they didn't like the smell of blood. But after a normal amount of fidgeting and nickering, they went along.

When they came into the ranch yard, the house was dark. Irene must have gone to bed. They led the horses up to the door. Olaf bellowed—"Irene!"—and dismounted. He began to untie the lashings that held Matthew in the saddle.

Dave helped him and they lifted Matt's body down, carried it into the house. Irene was there, and had lighted a lamp. Sheer terror showed in her eyes as she stared at Matthew.

Dave said: "He ain't dead, honey. He ain't even been hit."

"What's the matter with him, then?"

"I don't know."

They carried him to the long, horsehair sofa and laid him down. Dave started to turn. A sudden, uneasy feeling stirred him and he whirled. Matthew's eyes were open, staring at him. Dave grabbed Olaf's arm.

"Look!"

Olaf turned in surprise. He stared into Matthew's bitter, hating eyes for a moment, then began to laugh. He laughed until the tears coursed down his cheeks.

He roared: "He's had a stroke! He's paralyzed. But his mind is clear. Look at his eyes!" Apparently the possibilities this offered began to unroll before him.

Dave asked: "What you going to do with him?"

"I ain't going to kill him if that's what you mean. I'm going to keep him alive." He put his face down close to Matthew's. He said: "You hear that, Matt? I'm going to keep you for a pet."

Matthew's facial muscles twitched. It was plain that he was trying to speak. He couldn't and the knowledge distilled the bitterness in his eyes into more concentrated form.

Olaf grinned at him. "We're moving to the Wheel tomorrow, Matt. We'll take you back with us." He looked at Irene, and his tone became mocking. "I don't think you two have met." He postured ridiculously. "Mister Waymire, meet Missus Waymire."

Matthew's eyes looked faintly puzzled.

Olaf explained: "Ernie killed Al, Matt. Ernie's on the dodge for it. But before he left, he married Irene here. She's appointed me foreman of the Wheel. You see how it is now?"

Matthew's facial muscles twitched violently. At last something vital went out of them. He was helpless and he knew it. He was at the mercy of Olaf, and there was no mercy in Olaf. He knew that, too. He closed his eyes tightly and held them that way. Olaf laughed again.

Irene shuddered and ran to her room. Olaf went over and picked up Matthew. He carried him into his own bedroom and dropped him on the bed. When he came back out, he bellowed at Irene's closed door: "You take care of him! I'll sleep in the bunkhouse with the boys tonight. Tomorrow we'll have plenty of room."

Then he stalked outside, chuckling, and after a moment's hesitation Dave followed.

It was a strange cavalcade that came straggling into

Wheel headquarters at noon the following day. Olaf and Frank, grinning triumphantly, rode in the vanguard. Behind them, Irene drove a wagon loaded with personal effects. Bringing up the rear was the Hunnicutt buckboard. In the back Matthew, paralyzed, and Al, dead, rode side-by-side. Dave drove the buckboard. Trailing it and tied to it was a string of saddle horses tied, lead rope to tail, in a long line.

The sheriff, Nate Gunlock, was waiting at the Wheel, having been notified by Frank the previous night that Al and Matthew were dead. He came walking out from the house, and the crew streamed from the bunkhouse, following him.

Gunlock looked up at Olaf. "What's this?"

Olaf grinned. He jerked his head toward Irene. He said mockingly: "Meet Missus Ernie Waymire. Al's dead, but old Matt ain't. He needs good care. He's had a stroke. Missus Waymire's going to take care of him."

Gunlock scowled. "Looks to me like you're all moving in."

"We are. Hell, man, Missus Waymire's going to be busy with old Matt. She'll need someone to look after things. The Wheel is a big outfit. But I reckon Frank and Dave and me can look after it for her."

Gunlock chewed his lip thoughtfully. "I want to see Matt." He walked back to the buckboard. Anger stirred in his eyes. He said: "Did you have to put Al right beside him?"

Olaf couldn't seem to get the pleased grin off his face. "Why, Sheriff, you know, I never thought of that." He grunted at Frank and Dave: "Get him in the house."

Dave got down, walked around to the rear of the buckboard. Frank rode over and dismounted. He hitched at the two low-swung guns and reached for Matthew's feet. Gunlock pushed him aside. "I want to talk to Matthew."

Frank snarled: "He can't talk. He's paralyzed."

"I'll try."

Gunlock walked around to Matt's side of the buckboard. Matthew watched him. His eyes seemed to want to talk. But they were mute.

Gunlock said: "Ernie killed Al and you had a stroke. What were you trying to do to Ernie, Matt? Push him into killing you?"

The muscles of Matthew's face twitched. His eyes were frantic.

Gunlock said: "Ernie's a good man, and so was Al. I guess, if you'd been more of a father to them, this wouldn't have happened." He stared at Matthew thoughtfully. "I always thought I'd be glad when something happened to you, Matt. But I ain't. I'm sorry for you. You got nothing to do but think now, have you? You got to lay there and watch Olaf take over your ranch."

The eyes were desperate and the stricken man's face twitched frantically.

Gunlock shook his head. "You're tryin' to tell me to stop Olaf, ain't you? I can't do it, Matt. I talked to the preacher that tied Ernie and Irene last night. It's legal enough. Al's dead. You're helpless and Ernie's gone. There ain't a thing in the world to stop Ernie's wife from bringing her family and moving to the Wheel." He looked at Matthew a moment longer. Finally, turning away, he said: "I'm sorry, Matt."

One of the Wheel cowpunchers stopped him, drew him aside. Dave, lifting Matthew, couldn't help but hear: "I'm quitting, Nate. Who do I see?"

"Olaf," Gunlock said. "He's the boss now.

"That's what I figured. I guess I'll go see him now."

The cowpuncher walked over to where Olaf stood. Half a dozen others followed him.

Dave went into the house, lugging Matt's head and shoulders. He and Frank carried the man into his own bedroom and laid him down on the bed. Irene came in. There was pity in her face as she looked at Matt. Dave thought it was strange about women, strange how quickly they forgot an injury or a wrong, strange how they could feel sympathy for the one who had wronged them.

He guessed all women weren't like that. He stared at Irene, fussing over Matthew. He was seeing her with different eyes today. She had matured in the last couple of days. She was a woman now, not a girl.

She was the only one of the Hunnicutt tribe that amount to a damn. Dave himself hadn't even had the guts to refuse to go along with a steal like this. Maybe a word from him wouldn't bust it wide open, but it would give Gunlock something to work on.

Instinct told him: *Let it ride. See what happens.* He grunted with self-contempt as he went out the door. That was the easy way. But he knew that was the way he'd do it. Family loyalty was a strong tie, especially strong in the Hunnicutt family. He couldn't break it.

Outside, Olaf was paying off the crew with money he had found in old Matt's office. When that was done and they had left, only the cook and Ramón Ortiz were left.

Dave squatted against the bunkhouse wall beside Ramón and asked: "You're the only one that stayed. Why?"

Ramón grinned cheerfully. "I am a cowpuncher here. If I leave, I will be something less than that. I think I stay for that."

It was all right with Dave. Dave was sweet on Ramón's sister, Rosalia. Another tie wouldn't hurt a thing. He got up. "You won't regret it, Ramón."

"I know I will not. I am sure of that." Ramón grinned at him.

Dave and Frank and Ramón began the task of unpacking the wagon and carting the stuff into the house. The Hunnicutt horses were turned out with the Wheel remuda. Gunlock watched, apparently reluctant to leave.

Dave asked: "Going after Ernie?"

"Have to." Gunlock swung up to saddle and stared down at Dave. " 'Luck," he said, and rode away toward Cedrino.

Dave thought: *He'll stall around for three days gathering a posse. He'll comb the desert first, then move up to the Spanish Peaks. But by that time Ernie'll be clear to Colorado, and Gunlock knows it.*

Well, it wasn't essential to Olaf's plan that Ernie be caught. In fact, Olaf would probably like it just as well if Ernie wasn't caught. He wouldn't come back, that was sure. Coming back would only put a noose around his neck.

Dave marveled at the ease with which luck had dumped the Wheel into Olaf's lap. A foolproof plan. One that couldn't misfire.

Still, he couldn't feel entirely comfortable about it. He couldn't entirely banish the odd feeling of uneasiness that lingered in his mind.

Apparently Olaf couldn't, either, for when supper was over, he called Dave over to the corral where they wouldn't be overheard. He said: "We need a crew. Six or eight at least. Take a pack horse and head down east to the Cherokee Strip or south into the Panhandle. I don't want an ordinary crew. I want a gun crew."

VIII

Relentlessly Ernie Waymire pushed back toward the Spanish Peaks all the first day, reaching the little mining town of Río de Oro at nightfall. He halted long enough to purchase a pack horse and a load of supplies, then rode out again.

He camped that night in the timber, built a fire, and cooked his dinner, then rolled up in his blankets. Sleep should have come easy, for he was utterly exhausted. But it did not. He kept thinking of Irene, his wife now, and he kept thinking of Olaf at the Wheel.

His anger was all the more terrible because it was helpless anger. His head began to ache again. Sometime before midnight, he dropped off to sleep.

When he awoke in the morning, he cooked breakfast and mounted. All that day he climbed steadily, and at night camped at the foot of one of the Spanish Peaks. Here, at this high altitude, snow still lay banked in the shady ravines, its surface black with dust. Ernie shot an elk calf and dressed it out. He fried a couple of good-size steaks for his supper.

The anger that had smoldered in him all day broke out again. He had to fight himself to keep from turning around, from starting back.

Again, at night, he lay awake, his mind relentlessly searching for some gap in Olaf's planning. There wasn't any.

On the following morning, he turned north, toward the Colorado border. He covered 200 miles in a little more than a week, but every time he passed through a town he became wary. He looked with suspicion on every man who gave him a second glance.

He spent his evenings now practicing with his gun. At first he practiced only his draw, but, as time went on and his speed improved, he began to practice with live ammunition.

Ernie had never given much thought to guns. He could shoot, as could almost everyone he knew. Beyond reasonable accuracy, he'd had no desire to learn. It was different now. His life might at any time depend upon how quickly he could draw his gun, how quickly and how accurately he could shoot.

To his surprise, he found that he had a natural bent for guns. He amazed himself occasionally by both his speed and his accuracy. He could break a clod in mid-air with a single shot, drawing and shooting with a single smooth motion only after the clod had left his hand.

When he came into Cordova, Colorado, in mid-afternoon one day, nearly three weeks had passed since he had left the Wheel. Cordova was not much different from a dozen towns he had passed through on the way. Perhaps a little bigger. That was all.

He stabled his horses and headed for a saloon. His clothes were travel-stained and a stubble of whiskers covered his face. He had lost nearly fifteen pounds. In his eyes was a sort of restrained fury as he banged through the batwings of the first saloon he came to, and strode to the bar.

At this time of day, the place was nearly deserted. A fat, mustached Mexican bartender was behind the bar. A couple of men were standing in front of it. Ernie ordered beer.

He drank it, and ordered another. While he was drinking it, one of the men left the saloon without a glance at him. The other studied him covertly in the backbar mirror. Ernie felt the stir of some wild instinct that had grown and matured in him during his weeks of running.

He began to think about the man who had left so suddenly, tried to remember what the man had looked like. The instinct of warning grew in him.

He paid for his beer and had started for the door when the batwings banged open. Three men crowded in.

One of them yelled: "That's him! Don't let him get away! He's worth a thousand bucks down in New Mexico!"

Ernie's gun was in his hand. He couldn't remember how it got there. He put a bullet into the floor in front of the nearest man. He yelled: "The next will be higher!"

He came around in a half turn. The bartender was leveling a double-barreled shotgun from behind the bar. Ernie flung a shot at him, showered his face with sharp splinters from the bar. The man who had been at the bar slowly raised his hands.

The bartender growled: "No wonder he's worth a thousand. It'd be worth more than that to take him." He held his hands above his head. The shotgun had fallen somewhere behind the bar.

Maybe this was what Ernie had needed, this tight and touchy moment. For an instant he wasn't sure but what one of the three at the door would make a play.

He said harshly: "Let go of your guns. Now! Let go of them! You're not going to get me, so don't try."

He waited, watching them, watching their nerve break. Guns clattered on the floor. Ernie made a compelling motion with his gun barrel.

"Over by the bar," he said. "Lie down on the floor. I didn't ask you to make this try for me. I'll make you sorry you did it if you don't move."

He watched them as they surlily obeyed. He thought of

his horse, of his pack animal down at the livery barn. Nearly two blocks away. He'd never make it to them, nor make it out of town with them. The horses would have to be saddled. That would take too long.

He backed out of the door with the final warning: "Don't hurry after me. Somebody'll get hurt next time."

There was a big black gelding racked in front of the saloon. A little flashy and easy to spot, but the best horse at the rack, and Ernie had to have the best.

His mind was racing and his time was ticking away. This was the way it began. Dodgers had gone out all over the West. There wasn't a place he could hide from them. He was innocent of any crime, but he was about to become guilty of horse stealing.

Sooner or later, he'd be guilty of murder. It could have happened back there in the saloon. It could happen here, now, in this Cordova street. It could happen five miles from town if this sheriff's posse caught up with him.

But wherever it happened, it was inevitable. Sooner or later, Ernie would have to kill to preserve his freedom. And then it wouldn't matter whether he were guilty of killing Al and Matthew or not. He'd be a murderer anyway.

His decision was made as he untied the black and swung to saddle. He turned the animal south.

He hit the edge of town at a dead run. He could hear the confused shouts in the town behind him. He relaxed a little and eased up on the black. The animal slowed to a mile-eating lope. There'd be no hasty pursuit. They'd take fifteen or twenty minutes to get organized, to round up men and horses. So he had a little time.

He used it in running in a steady, straight line. Time enough later for evasive tactics. He glanced up at the sun, guessing the time at close to four o'clock. It wouldn't be dark until about eight, but the moon wouldn't rise until about ten.

Ernie figured, if he could stay away from them until dark, he could lose them altogether between dark and moonrise. For yet another fifteen minutes he kept the horse at a steady lope, holding a straight and direct line toward the south. Off to his right were some low hills, and in the distance the snow-clad peaks of the Divide.

He knew what it was like to be hunted now, and he didn't like it. It had put the decision up to him in a way he couldn't ignore or evade. It was a choice now, between a losing fight back in Cedrino or a losing fight, lasting longer perhaps but just as inevitable, up here in the north.

It was the difference between death when knowing he was guilty of no wrong doing, or of death, knowing that he had killed innocent men in the process of keeping his freedom. It was really no choice at all, for in either case the end was the same.

Ernie heard a distant shot behind him, but he didn't smile. That shot may have been at a coyote, or a deer, or at an imagined movement. It told Ernie, though, that the men behind him were dangerous. They were dangerous because they were scared—scared and excited. They weren't manhunters, most of them. Just men of the town, pressed into service by a sheriff who probably was excited himself.

He estimated that the shot was no more than a couple of miles back of him. That meant either that they had got organized quicker than he had thought they would, or that they were pushing their horses too hard. He touched the black with his spurs, and the animal responded instantly, breaking into a smooth, free-flowing run.

With no more than a couple of miles separating pursued and pursuers, there was no leeway for evasive tactics anyway, so Ernie slacked the reins and let the horse run. He glanced down at the saddle, and was surprised and pleased to find a rifle jammed snugly into the boot. He withdrew it and jacked open the action. It was loaded.

An hour passed, with no apparent increase or decrease in the distance between him and the posse. At intervals, he let his horse slow to a walk, and a couple of times he stopped entirely, allowing the animal enough time to resume his normal breathing cadence.

This care of his horse must have paid off, because as the sun sank behind the snow-clad peaks to the westward he heard another shot. This one had come from almost double the distance behind him than the first had. Not only that, but his horse was not entirely played out, and with reasonable care should carry him throughout the night.

Immediately he turned right, entering the hills. At midnight, he was forty miles south of Cordova and knew that at last he had shaken off pursuit. Since he was wanted in New Mexico, they probably had not expected him to ride south. They had figured his southerly direction to be a ruse, and had expected him to turn back north again as soon as darkness fell. That would explain his losing the posse so easily.

He watered his weary horse and picketed the animal in a lush meadow of mountain hay. He had no food for himself, so he took a long drink of water and rolled himself in his blankets.

And for the first time in many days, he slept as soon as his head touched the saddle. . . .

Daylight found him riding, refreshed, but ravenously hungry. He shot a deer, dressed it, and loaded it on his saddle. At an outlying ranch, he traded most of it for a little coffee and flour. He kept traveling.

His horse threw a shoe on the third day. Ernie had no money left, so he roped a horse out of a bunch he found, and turned the black loose. He was careful to steal horses off the range, so that he would not be trailed by the reports of stolen horses.

He avoided towns, and replenished his supplies at outlying ranches, usually by bringing in dressed game on his saddle to exchange for them. There came a day when he sighted the Spanish Peaks in the distance, and at nightfall camped at their base.

The next night found him at the edge of the desert, awaiting darkness before attempting the ride into Cedrino. The running was over, and the fighting was about to begin.

Saturday night. From the bandstand in the plaza came the brassy strains of a march, muted by distance. Rosalia Ortiz slipped a shawl about her shoulders preparatory to stepping out into the street. The door opened behind her.

A voice said: "Blow out the lamp and lock the door."

She whirled. "Ernie!"

He stepped across the room and blew out the lamp. Rosalia locked the door. Moonlight streamed in the window. Ernie came over to her. He was gaunt and unshaven. His eyes burned in their sockets.

Rosalia cried: "You should not have come back!"

"I got tired of running." He stared down at her. "How much of what they accuse me of do you believe?"

There was no hesitation in her. "None of it."

"What do they accuse me of now? When I left it was killing Al and Matthew."

"But Matthew isn't dead."

"What?"

"He had a stroke or something. He's out at the Wheel

and Irene Hunnicutt is taking care of him."

"Then he can tell Gunlock how it really happened."

Rosalia shook her head. "He's paralyzed. He can't speak."

"And Olaf? Is he at the Wheel?"

"He and Frank and Dave. And four or five hired gunmen. The crew quit as soon as the Hunnicutts moved in. All except Ramón. He tells me what goes on out there."

Ernie smiled. "Then Olaf isn't sure of himself. Because if he was, he wouldn't bother with gunmen."

Rosalia said bitterly: "He gives a good imitation of being sure of himself."

But Ernie was chuckling. "Will you fix me something to eat? And will you let me sleep here tonight?"

"Of course." Rosalia started toward the kitchen.

Ernie was mumbling: "There's a flaw somewhere. There's a flaw in Olaf's plan. If there wasn't, he wouldn't have hired that kind of a crew."

Rosalia felt a stir of panic. "There is a flaw all right, but you will not find it because they will find you first." She returned to him, begged frantically: "Ernie, please! Go away. You will have the whole country to fight, and one man can't do it. They'll catch you and they'll. . . ." She couldn't go on.

Ernie was laughing softly. That surprised Rosalia. He should have been bitter; he should have been afraid. She shrugged, and turned away toward the kitchen. Perhaps she loved him more because he had returned. But she was afraid she would not be able to love him for long. No one man could live for long against the odds that Ernie Waymire faced.

Rosalia dropped a steak into a smoking skillet and began to cry, silently so that Ernie would not hear.

IX

Days passed slowly for Irene Hunnicutt. For most of her life she had kept house for her father and brothers, no small task in itself. Now, however, she not only kept house at the Wheel for them, but also cared for Matthew.

He was totally helpless. Only his sight and his hearing were unimpaired. She washed him, fed him, shaved him. She read to him from whatever books and newspapers she was able to find.

Often she lied to Olaf, making him believe that Matthew was asleep, saving Matthew the misery of Olaf's gloating. Remorse tortured Irene, remorse for the part she had played in Matthew's downfall and Ernie's outlawry.

She had no hope whatever that things would ever be different. Nor could she change them. Her word would be of no value against that of Olaf and Frank and Dave. She resolved, however, that she would stay here at the Wheel for only as long as Matthew lived. When he was gone, she would leave, would try to find another life for herself somewhere.

One hot morning about a month after moving to the Wheel, Irene found a copy of Shakespeare's *Midsummer Night's Dream* lying on a bench in front of the bunkhouse. Since all of the crew was gone, she decided to borrow it for the day, to read it to Matthew.

When she took it into the house, Matthew was awake. Irene pulled a chair toward the bed, sat down, and smiled at him. Whatever he had done during his life, whoever he had hurt, he was paying for it now.

Irene suddenly realized that she didn't hate Matthew any longer. He had hurt Ernie, had indirectly brought about all that had happened to all of them, yet *he* was paying the highest price.

She asked: "Would you like me to read you this?" She showed him the book so that he could read the title. Matthew blinked his eyes. Irene said: "It's a shame you can't talk. I never know if you like what I read to you or not. I guess, if you don't, you just have to suffer through it, don't you?"

Matthew blinked twice. There was a curious intensity in his glance. His face worked as though he were trying to speak. Irene laid the book aside.

"You're trying to tell me something, aren't you?"

Again Matthew blinked.

Irene asked: "Are you hungry?"

Matthew blinked twice.

Irene, puzzled, said: "I wish I could think of some way to figure out what you want."

Matthew's face worked violently. He managed to utter a small croak. It was obvious that he was intensely excited, and angry, too. Suddenly he began to blink his eyes, rapidly, ceaselessly. Irene's eyes widened. Matthew stopped blinking. Then he blinked once, waited, blinked again. His look at Irene was intense, pleading. He blinked twice in rapid succession, waited, and did it again.

Irene felt a sudden soaring excitement. She said: "Why, you're trying to talk to me! Yes is one blink, no is two, is that it?"

Matthew blinked once. The relief in his eyes was almost pitiful. Irene got up and went to the door. She wandered through the house, making sure that Olaf and Frank and Dave were gone. When she came back to Matthew's room, she went to the window and peered out. Then she returned to the bedside.

She said: "You can answer questions if I can think of the right ones to ask." She realized that she still held the book in her hand. "Do you want me to read you this book now?"

Matthew blinked twice.

Irene asked: "Later?"

One blink.

Irene put down the book. "Do you want to talk?"

Matthew signified: "Yes."

Irene realized suddenly that although she could now communicate to some degree with Matthew, she still could not know what was in his mind, or know his desires. Only through questions put to him by herself could she communicate with him at all. It would take patience, lots of patience.

Another realization struck her with stunning force. Now Matthew would be able to talk to the sheriff, if only by this primitive form of communication. With Matthew's backing Irene's story, it would now be possible to oust Olaf from the Wheel. It would be possible to clear Ernie of the murder charge from which he was fleeing! Her word, backed up by that of Matthew, would be more than sufficient.

She said: "Would you like to talk to the sheriff?"

Matthew blinked once. His eyes showed great relief.

Irene asked: "You hate me, don't you? For what I've done?"

He blinked twice. His eyes, which at first had been so hating and so hard, were not so now.

Irene felt tears smarting in her own eyes. She asked: "Do you hate Ernie?"

Again Matthew signed: "No."

"Would you want Ernie back here at the Wheel?"

Matthew indicated that he did.

"But you wouldn't want me here, too?"

Matthew hesitated at the way her question was phrased, although Irene did not know that. Finally he blinked twice. Irene misunderstood.

She said—"I guess I can't blame you."—turning away. She did not see the violent twitching of his face as he sought to make her understand. She was looking out the window.

She turned back toward the bed. "Trying to get the sheriff out here will be dangerous. Olaf has hired a new crew. They're a hard-looking lot and they all wear guns." She thought for a moment. "I can't go into town. Olaf wouldn't let me. He still doesn't trust me. I can't send a letter, either." Suddenly she thought of Ramón Ortiz. She asked: "Can we trust Ramón?"

For a moment Matthew stared at her, his eyes both thoughtful and doubtful. Finally he blinked once.

Irene almost smiled. She said: "You think so, but you're not sure, is that it?"

Matthew blinked immediately.

Irene thought of the sour-faced old cook. She asked: "How about the cook? Do you trust him?"

Matthew's answer was an unhesitating yes.

Yet his eyes seemed to want to tell her something further. Irene thought about that. She could not remember the cook's ever leaving the ranch, at least in the few weeks she had been at Wheel.

She asked: "Does the cook ever go to town?"

Matthew blinked twice.

Irene frowned. If the cook was not in the habit of going to town, a sudden trip might arouse Olaf's suspicion. She looked at Matthew. "Do you think it would be better to send the cook after the sheriff?"

Matthew blinked twice.

"You want me to send Ramón, then?"

Matthew indicated that he did.

Irene said: "All right. I'll talk to him the first chance I get. You go to sleep. You look tired."

She went out of the room, closing the door quietly behind her. She was conscious of her shaking hands. She was conscious of an over-powering tension. She began to realize that there was infinite danger in what she had learned today. If Olaf got even an inkling that Matthew could talk, Matthew would be dead in an hour.

She was also aware that Olaf, having tasted the power and wealth the Wheel gave him, would kill without compunction to hold the Wheel. He had used Irene herself, his own daughter, to obtain the Wheel. He would use her, even sacrifice her, to keep it. So there was danger not only to Matthew, but to herself as well.

She could see now that, if she had been less under Olaf's thumb at the beginning, this could never have happened. It was her own greed that had tripped her up, had made her fall in with Olaf's plans. If she had done what Ernie wanted her to, to begin with, all would have been well.

Desperately she wished she had gone away with him when he first asked her. What would it have mattered if she'd had to live in a one-room, dirt-floored shack? She'd have had Ernie, and she'd have had the future. Now she had nothing, not even her self-respect.

Despair ran through her thoughts. She went out onto the portico and sank into a chair. Heat blazed down into the yard, rising in shimmering waves, distorting the horizon, every object in view. Irene pushed a damp strand of dark hair away from her forehead.

She had lost weight in these last few weeks, but it detracted in no way from her beauty. There was a haunting, hollow look to her cheeks. A pulse beat visibly in her throat.

The Wheel, she realized, no longer meant anything to her. What was it, when all was said and done? A ranch house, and a plain ranch house at that. Land—lots of land—stretching toward the horizon as far as the eye could see, and even beyond that. Cattle. Thousands of cattle.

It was something else to Irene, and it would always be that. It was a man's life sacrificed on the altar of greed. It was another's man's health, also sacrificed. It was Ernie, gone from her forever. It was her own happiness, as remote from her now as Ernie was.

Yet in righting this wrong that had been done, even if it should cost her life, a measure of self-respect and happiness might be regained. She thought about that for a while, and gradually her composure returned. Gradually her despair lessened.

She went through the house to the kitchen. Seran, the cook, was kneading bread dough on the table. His sleeves were rolled up to the elbows. He frowned at her irritably.

Irene said: "You hate me, and I can't blame you. But there is a way out of this. Matthew can speak."

Seran's voice was harsh. "You're lying. He's paralyzed."

Irene said: "But he can blink his eyes. Once is yes, twice no."

Seran took his hands out of the dough and began to wipe them on his apron.

Irene said: "Go in to him. See if what I say isn't so."

He looked at her suspiciously. "Why you telling me this?"

"Because I need your help. Come into his room with me, and I'll tell you why in front of him. You can ask him if what I say is true."

Seran followed her through the house to Matthew's room. Matthew was still awake.

Irene said: "I told Seran that you could speak. Tell him if it is true."

Matthew blinked once.

Irene felt a strange, weird excitement. She said: "I need his help. I can't go to the bunkhouse to see Ramón. It is too dangerous to you for me to risk getting Olaf suspicious. He'd kill you in a minute if he thought you could talk."

Matthew blinked.

Irene turned to the cook. She said: "We want to send Ramón to Cedrino for the sheriff. We want to get the sheriff out here to talk to Matthew. But he must come when Olaf is away. He must not be seen here. Now, ask Matthew if what I have said is the truth."

Seran's voice asked harshly: "Is it, boss?"

Matthew blinked once.

Still Seran seemed suspicious. He grumbled: "How do I know he don't mean no?"

"Ask him some of your own questions."

"I will." The cook turned to the man on the bed. "How long I been working for you, boss? Five years?"

Matthew blinked twice.

"Ten?" asked Seran. Again Matthew signed: "No."

Seran asked: "Twenty-three?"

Matthew considered that for a moment, finally blinking once in assent.

Seran whistled. "Lordy! This is plumb uncanny."

Irene said sharply: "You are to tell no one about it, do you understand? Not even Ramón."

"Sure, ma'am. Sure." He turned to Matthew, asking doubtfully: "You reckon this here woman is all right?"

Matthew signed: "Yes."

Seran turned away. "I guess that's good enough for me."

Irene heard a shout in the yard, the pound of hoofs. She ran to the window. Olaf, tall and burly in the saddle, rode into the yard at the head of three of his gunslingers. Frank rode beside him, gun hung, scowling as was his habit.

Irene turned from the window. She said: "Get back to the kitchen. Try to see Ramón tonight."

The cook shuffled out.

Irene smiled at Matthew. "It will be all right. It will be all right, won't it?" It was as though she sought assurance, support from the helpless old man on the bed. He blinked at her once, and she thought, if he could smile, he would he smiling now.

She went outside and watched Olaf and Frank unsaddle. The crew slouched into the bunkhouse, and Olaf and Frank came toward the house. Olaf seemed about to speak to her, but just then another rider came pounding into the yard. It was another of the tough crew, one named Lew Murray. He rode directly to the house.

He said: "Boss, what'd you say Ernie Waymire looked like?"

Olaf described Ernie quickly.

Murray grunted: "Then I seen him. I seen him not an hour ago. He was stopped at Apache Springs, watering his horse."

Irene looked at Olaf. His face grew red, darkened until it was a deep brick color. He roared: "Red! Sam! Miguel! Saddle up! We're going hunting! By God, we're going hunting!"

The crew tumbled out of the bunkhouse. Olaf and Lew and Frank ran toward the corral. In less than three minutes all six of them thundered out of the yard, heading toward Apache Springs.

And Irene was helpless, totally helpless. Or was she? Olaf and Frank would be gone all night if necessary, chasing Ernie. There could be no better time to go to Cedrino after the sheriff than now! And since Ramón was not here, Irene would go herself.

She ran into the house, into Matthew's' room. She cried: "One of the crew has seen Ernie! They've all gone after him. Ramón isn't in yet, so I'm going after the sheriff."

Without waiting to see what Matthew's reaction would be, she fled from the room. She did not even bother to change her clothes. She ran across the yard, snatched her side-saddle from the corral fence. Roping a horse expertly from the bunch, she flung the saddle onto him and cinched it down. Then she was spurring wildly in the direction of Cedrino.

As she rode, she began to pray. Not for herself, but for Ernie. With six determined men chasing him, Ernie was the one who needed her prayers.

X

Night had come when Irene Hunnicutt rode her exhausted horse down the narrow, rutted street of Cedrino. The moon was rising from the horizon, a yellow, enlarged ball that put a warm light upon the town. She could hear a soft Mexican voice singing somewhere, and the sound of a guitar.

She passed Rosalia Ortiz's restaurant, and glanced in the window. Her brother Dave was at one of the tables, talking to Rosalia. She hurried past, hoping he would not glance out into the street.

At the sheriff's office she dismounted stiffly. She pushed open the door, breathing a sigh of relief. Tall, gaunt old Nate Gunlock sat at his desk with his feet up. He was smoking a long black cigar with every evidence of enjoyment. Irene guessed that he had just come from the restaurant.

He got to his feet hastily when he saw her. "Miss Hunnicutt . . . er . . . Missus Waymire!" There was surprise in his tone. "What are you doing in town? I thought. . . ."

Irene had no time to find out what he thought. It didn't matter anyway. She said urgently: "I haven't much time, so listen to me carefully. Ernie didn't kill Al. My brother Frank did that."

The sheriff said grimly: "I've suspected that Ernie didn't have anything to do with it. That's why I haven't been pressing the hunt for him too hard. Can you prove it?"

"Yes. I was there. Also, I can communicate with Matthew. He blinks his eyes to give yes and no answers. I want you to ride out to the Wheel with me tonight and talk to him. I want you to clear Ernie."

Gunlock had come to his feet. "Well, I guess so!"

"It's dangerous for you, and for me as well. I know Olaf. He's had a taste of owning the Wheel and he won't give it up."

"Let me worry about Olaf." There was something grim in the sheriff's tone.

Irene let what she had so determinedly kept pushed back in her thoughts all the way to town come out now. She said: "Ernie's back. Olaf knows it. He and Frank and four of those gunslingers Dave hired are hunting him." She put her face down into her hands, shaking, but not crying. She was holding onto herself with grim desperation. If she let go now. . . .

Gunlock gripped her shoulders. "Don't worry . . . don't worry. It won't help Ernie a bit. Ernie's been running over a month. And he's smart. He's learned a lot of the tricks of staying away from pursuit by now." He started for the door. "Wait here a minute. I want Kirby along on this ride. I want another witness, in case." He was gone out the door.

Irene sat down and clenched her hands together. Her thoughts kept screaming: *Hurry! Hurry!*

It seemed an eternity before Gunlock and Kirby came back. Gunlock came over and touched her shoulders. He said: "We've got a few minutes to wait. I sent to the stable after our horses, and for a fresh one for you." He went back to his desk and sat down.

Oliver Kirby, elegant and somber-faced, lounged against the wall.

Gunlock asked: "Will you tell me the whole story now? It will save time after we get to the Wheel."

"All right."

Irene began at the beginning, with Olaf's corrosive hatred of Matthew. She outlined the trap Olaf had set for Ernie, by using her as bait. She did not spare herself in the recital. But when she came to the part where she had fallen in love with Ernie, she began to cry.

A small Mexican boy stuck his head in the door. "*Señores,* the horses. I bring them."

Gunlock stood up. He tossed the boy a coin.

Outside, he helped Irene to her side-saddle, then mounted himself. Kirby mounted, and the three went out of town at a fast trot.

Out on the road, Gunlock lifted his horse to a slow, rocking lope. Irene was tired. As they rode, she finished her story, told about the shooting, about Olaf's slugging Ernie, about the later developments after they had discovered that Matthew was alive.

After that, she was silent. Each moment was an eternity, and the hours dragged endlessly. But at last they raised the lights of the Wheel ranch house ahead.

Irene and Kirby waited outside the fringe of darkness, while Gunlock went forward afoot to scout the place. Only one of the crew was present besides Ramón Ortiz, and both of them were in the bunkhouse. Gunlock came back. Silently the three rode in. They tied their horses behind the house.

While Irene waited, Gunlock and Kirby, guns drawn, went into the bunkhouse. There was a sharp flurry of action. Then Gunlock and Kirby came out. Ramón Ortiz followed, dragging the unconscious gunman. They carried him to the door of the root cellar, tied his hands and feet, and took him down the stairs into the cellar.

Irene led the three of them into the house. She was calculating the odds now, and found them not so unfavorable as before. There was Gunlock; there was Kirby. Ramón and the cook could be trusted. And there was herself. Five in all.

Against them would be the six who were hunting Ernie, when and if they returned. Gunmen all of them. Dave was undoubtedly still in town. Ernie was. . . .

Irene shuddered. Her lips moved in silent prayer.

Ramón went into the kitchen after Seran, the cook. Irene led Gunlock and Kirby to Matthew's bedroom. He was asleep. She shook him gently. He opened his eyes. He looked at Gunlock and Kirby.

Irene said: "I've told the whole story to Mister Gunlock. I'll tell them again, now, and they want you to blink your eyes once to indicate that what I'm saying is the truth."

Gunlock looked at Matthew. "Do you understand, Matt?"

Matthew blinked.

In Irene was a feeling of desperation. In spirit, she was with Ernie, fleeing across the desert, with six determined and ruthless men at his heels. If they caught him. . . .

Resolutely she began to talk. At intervals she would stop,

and Gunlock or Kirby would ask Matthew: "Is that the way it was, Matt?"

Matthew would blink to indicate that what she said was true.

Ramón and the cook watched from the door. There was a gap in the story. None of them knew how Matthew and Al Waymire had come to be at the rendezvous that fateful Saturday night. That was a secret locked inside of Matthew. Only he, or the dead Al, could tell that, and neither could talk.

At last it was finished. Then the waiting began.

Midnight passed. Seran went to the kitchen and shortly returned with a big pot of black coffee. After a while, Matthew dropped off to sleep. They filed out of his room to the big living room and sat around, silently waiting.

Once, Irene screamed at the sheriff: "Do something! Do something! Ernie's being hunted. They'll kill him! You've got to stop it!" She began to sob brokenly.

Gunlock came over and patted her shoulder awkwardly. "There ain't nothing we can do, honey. We ain't got a chance of finding that bunch out on the desert tonight. If we did find 'em out there, we couldn't do anything. We've got to wait for them here and try and surprise them. It's the only chance we got."

They blew out the lamps and waited in darkness. Gunlock asked: "Irene, do you know why old Matt and your father hated each other?"

She shook her head. She realized at once that Gunlock could not see her, and she said: "No. I guess nobody knows except the two of them."

Kirby cleared his throat. "Maybe Matt would want it known. I don't think there's any point in secrecy now."

Gunlock whistled. "Do you know?"

"Yes." Kirby's chair *creaked* and he cleared his throat. "I was practicing law in a little Kansas town when I first knew Matt and Olaf. Matt wasn't much different than he is now. He was hard as nails. A religious man . . . too much so. He thought all forms of pleasure were the works of the devil. His wife was a good woman, but she was different than Matt."

Irene interrupted: "Was she Ernie's mother?"

"Yes. She shriveled, living with Matt. She liked people, dancing, music. She liked everything." His tone was soft, reminiscent. Irene had the thought: *Why, Mister Kirby loved her!*

Kirby went on: "She bore him two sons, Al and Ernie. As soon as Al was weaned, she ran away with Olaf Hunnicutt."

Suddenly Irene could see it. The reason for Matt's undying hatred of Olaf. But she had not heard it all. She had not yet learned why Olaf hated Matt.

Kirby coughed. His voice was lower pitched, more intense. He said: "Matt followed, of course. He left the two babies with a neighbor woman and followed. He caught up with them at Abilene. They were registered at a hotel as man and wife."

Gunlock's voice was gruff. "Were you there?"

"I got there a little too late. You see, I loved Matt's wife, too, although she didn't know it. She would never have known it from me. But I was afraid for her. I knew Matt. I knew his violent temper."

He cleared his throat. He waited for a long time. The silence grew uncomfortable.

Finally Gunlock said: "What happened?"

Kirby's voice was different, strained. He said: "Matt found out where they were. He went storming into the hotel room after them. He had a gun. He told Olaf he was going to kill him. He laughed. He said there wasn't a jury in the country would convict him for it. I guess he was about to do it. . . ."

Kirby stopped again. Irene wished she could see his face. She wondered if it was as tortured as his voice.

Finally Kirby said hoarsely: "Mary tried to stop Matt. She grappled with him."

Gunlock said: "And he shot her?"

"No. But it was just as bad. He struck her. He was blind with rage. He struck her in the face with his fist to knock her out of the way. She hit her head against a corner of the bed as she fell." His voice dropped to a whisper. "It killed her."

He went on, his voice stronger, showing anger now. "I burst into the room just as Matt struck her. I clubbed him with my gun barrel. But it was too late. She was dead."

Now everything was plain to Irene. It was a terrible story, but it explained a lot of things.

But Kirby wasn't through. He said, his voice singularly lifeless: "Olaf left town before Matthew came to. He came to Cedrino and settled. He married a local woman . . . your mother, Irene. But Matthew kept hunting him."

Gunlock asked: "Matt was cleared by the law, then?"

"Yes. They called it accidental death. It was that all right. Matt was a crazy man when he realized what he'd done. But he kept hunting Olaf. And at last he found him."

Gunlock said: "Didn't he try to kill him then?"

"No. A couple of years had passed. He'd cooled off. Maybe he'd begun to see that he'd been wrong, too. Or maybe he felt a sense of responsibility to his two sons. He didn't try to kill Olaf, but he couldn't stop hating him." Kirby lapsed into silence. After a long while, he said: "Olaf didn't stop hating Matt, either. Olaf really loved Mary, just as I did. Now Olaf's had his revenge."

Irene could not help thinking: *But you haven't.*

Apparently Gunlock had just thought of the same thing. He said: "Matt killed her, and both you and Olaf loved her. Didn't you hate Matt for killing her?"

Kirby got out of his chair and strode to the window. He stared out at the moonlit yard. At last he said: "Yes. I hated him." He turned around, facing Gunlock. The moon, shining on one side of his face, showed an almost fanatical intensity there. But his voice was calm, almost gentle. "Time softens everything. A man can't live his life out hating. I tried to think that perhaps Mary had forgiven Matt. I tried to tell myself that Matt was suffering, that he was paying for what he'd done."

A shout lifted out on the desert, distant and unreal. Gunlock sprang to his feet. "Here they come!"

Swiftly, with no confusion at all, Seran and Ramón took positions at two of the windows, resting their rifle barrels on the sills. Gunlock went to the front door, his Colt cocked in his hand. Irene, with Kirby forgotten now, went and stood beside him.

Olaf pounded into the yard, with Frank just behind him. Irene's lips moved with a prayer for Ernie. She heard Frank's steady cursing.

Olaf shouted: "Shut up, damn you! We'll catch him. We'll go out first thing in the morning and we'll run him down if it takes a month!"

All of the tension left Irene with painful abruptness. She could feel warm tears of relief flooding her eyes, running across her cheeks. She breathed: "Ernie's safe. Ernie's safe. Thank God."

Gunlock stepped out onto the porch. He called: "Frank!

I want you for the murder of Al Waymire!"

There was a flurry of confusion in the yard. Olaf shouted: "What the hell?" He spurred across the yard and brought his horse to a plunging halt before the sheriff. "Damn you, Gunlock, get out of here!"

Gunlock said: "Matthew talked. He said Frank killed Al. He told the whole story, Olaf."

Irene stood in the doorway, shivering with terror. At that moment she admired the sheriff tremendously. But he didn't know Olaf as she did. Olaf wouldn't give up. Olaf yanked his gun clear.

Gunlock's revolver spouted orange flame, and the horse, shot through the shoulders, sprang forward and pitched to his knees, throwing Olaf clear. From across the yard, flame laced from the barrels of Frank's two guns.

Frank yelled: "Let 'em have it, boys! This is what you were hired for!"

Gunlock came across the portico, running. He burst through the door and slammed it behind him. He yelled: "Get down, girl! Stay away from the windows and doors. The damned fools are going to fight!"

Irene remembered that she hadn't seen Kirby since they had first heard that shout out on the desert. She looked around the room. It was dark, lighted only by the moon glow filtering in through the open windows. But Kirby was not in the room.

She said, panic making her voice high: "Sheriff, where is Mister Kirby?"

At that instant, the shot boomed out. Inside the house it was reverberating and echoing. In Matthew's room. Irene ran toward the hallway that led to Matthew's bedroom. She almost ran into Kirby. He had a gun in his hand. Irene smelled the acrid smoke rising from its muzzle.

Kirby said carefully: "I'm your man, Sheriff. I just killed Matt."

XI

Complete knowledge of the desert surrounding the Wheel ranch house had enabled Ernie to stay away from Olaf and Frank and their riders. Once they rode past his hiding place in a dry arroyo so close that he could hear the breathing of their horses.

As soon as they had passed out of earshot that time, he had headed for Wheel headquarters. He approached through the horse pasture. 100 yards from the corral, he tied his horse to the fence, and approached on foot. He had no idea of what he hoped to accomplish by this, but he knew that whatever he did accomplish could not be done riding around on the desert.

At the Wheel was the key to clearing himself with the law—Irene. If he could talk to her, he might be able to find out what had actually happened the night Al was killed. Knowing precisely what had happened, perhaps he could then map some course of action.

He had no sooner reached the shadow of the corral, than Olaf and the others rode in.

Frank's steady cursing stirred the anger in Ernie. He heard Gunlock's call from the house. He saw the flurry of shots. And he heard the shot inside the house.

Gunlock's words had the same effect on Ernie as a deep draft of fiery liquor would have had. He felt the racing of his blood, a quickening of his breathing. He drew his Colt.

Olaf was running across the yard. The two guns in Frank's hands were still spitting at the house. Frank emptied his guns, then ducked into the shadow of the bunk-house to reload.

Frank, then, had killed Al. Frank was the one Ernie wanted first. Then Olaf. A figure broke away from the house, a figure almost white in the dim moonlight. Ernie could see that the man's hat was white. Oliver Kirby. What the hell was he doing out here?

Kirby headed around the house, but one of Olaf's gun crew, hiding there, threw a shot at him. He veered away, hesitated. Someone else, over behind the bunkhouse took another shot at him. Neither scored

Kirby broke into a run, this time heading directly across the yard toward the corral. He moved like a wraith through the dappled pattern that the cottonwoods cast.

Ernie waited. Someone else threw a hasty shot at Kirby, missed. The bullet cut chips of bark out of a corral pole an inch above Ernie's head. He ducked instinctively, swore instinctively.

A rifle *boomed* from the house, targeting on the flash of that last pistol shot. A man howled, and began to curse violently. Kirby would have run right past Ernie, but Ernie stuck out a foot and tripped him.

He sat down on Kirby, saying: "Where the hell you going? You figuring on walking clear to town?" He wanted to talk to Kirby. He wanted to know what was going on. He said: "How'd Gunlock know Frank Hunnicutt killed Al?"

The fright seemed to go out of the lawyer upon learning that this was Ernie, and not a Hunnicutt man. He said, turning his head: "Irene came into town tonight and told him. Gunlock and I came out and talked to Matthew."

"I thought he was paralyzed."

"He was. But he could blink his eyes. Irene worked it out so he could blink once for yes, twice for no."

"Then I'm in the clear. I'm free." Ernie failed to notice Kirby's use of the past tense.

Kirby twisted under him. "Can I go now?"

"I guess you can. But it's a hell of a long walk to town."

Kirby got up and dusted himself off with his hands. He picked up his hat and flapped it against a knee.

Ernie asked: "Who's in the house?"

"Gunlock and Irene, Seran and Ramón. Dave's in town. You can count him out of this. He has no stomach for fighting this fight. He never had."

"And Matthew's there, too?"

Kirby nodded.

Ernie said: "All right. Go on." This wasn't Kirby's fight, and besides that Kirby wasn't what you'd call a fighting man. Ernie didn't feel he had the right to ask him to stay. As an afterthought, he said: "My horse is tied a hundred yards or so down the pasture fence. Use him if you want."

He was thinking of the $200 Kirby had given him, thinking of the way Kirby had talked Gunlock into giving him a job. This wasn't much repayment, but it was all he could manage now.

Kirby scuttled away. As soon as he was a dozen yards from Ernie, he began to run. Ernie turned his attention back to the house. There was desultory rifle fire from the two front windows.

During his weeks of running, Ernie had figured out that it must have been Al who had trailed him to his meeting place with Irene. It must have been Al who had brought Matthew out that night. The knowledge that Al had betrayed him did not increase his love for Al. But Al was dead. You couldn't hate the dead for what they'd done. Maybe Al had had a reason for what he did.

Ernie was intensely aware that, if his presence were discovered by Olaf or Frank, he wouldn't last long. His horse was gone. If Olaf and Frank, and their gun crew, concentrated on Ernie instead of on the house, he wouldn't have a chance. It followed then, that what fighting he did would have to be done carefully.

He slid along in the shadow of the corral. Running, he crossed a spot of open ground in full moonlight. A man behind the root cellar moved aside slightly to give him room in the shadow. Ernie realized immediately that the man had mistaken him for one of the crew. He had his gun in his hand. He brought its barrel down in a slashing arc against the man's head, and caught him as he fell.

The man wore a battered, black felt hat, with the brim pulled down in front. Ernie eased him to the ground and traded hats with him. He took the man's gun out of its holster and tossed it up onto the roof of the cellar. The man's rifle followed.

The barn was next. Pulling the black hat down low on his face, Ernie ran across to it. He was grinning a little, amused that he was drawing no fire. The hat had done the trick.

A man stood at the corner of the barn, peering at the house. As Ernie approached, he brought his gun up and fired. Ernie could hear the solid sound the bullet made biting into the adobe bricks of the house. Ernie slugged him from behind. The man pitched forward into the bright moonlight, and lay still. Ernie backed away from this corner and walked clear around the barn. Coming out on the other side, he ran across to the shelter of the bunkhouse.

There was no mistaking the man here. Frank Hunnicutt. Slight and dark. Sharp-faced. Two holsters, both tied down, and a gun in each hand. This had to be different.

Ernie stood and looked at him for a moment. He was

thinking of Al, of all the good times they'd had as kids. He was thinking of the way Al and he had sort of stood together against old Matthew. Ernie felt as cold as ice. He'd never done this before, but there was only one way to do it.

He called softly: "Frank. It's Ernie. Turn around and see if you can give me what you gave Al."

Frank froze for the briefest instant. Then it seemed as though every muscle and nerve in his body went tight. He whirled.

Ernie waited until he came fully around. Why, he couldn't have said. Frank wouldn't have given him the same chance. Frank's left-hand gun went off, although it was not even pointing at Ernie. The right-hand gun shot off a blue reflection of moonlight. Ernie's finger tightened down on the trigger. A blow struck his shoulder and drove him back. He staggered, recovered his balance, and fired again.

He could have saved that one. Frank was crumpling to the ground, limp, dead as he fell.

Ernie heard Olaf's bellow: "Frank! What the hell?"

He heard running feet. His shoulder felt numb. He backed away. Automatically transferring his gun to his left hand, he whirled and ran.

He went around the corner of the bunkhouse, running full tilt into another man, another of the crew. Ernie stuck his gun in the man's belly. He said harshly: "Horses in the corral. I'd pull out if I was you. Frank's dead, and two of the crew are out cold. Take a tip, friend, and run."

He let the man go by and gave him a little push. He watched to be sure the man would run. The man made a straight line for the corral.

Ernie went on around the bunkhouse, to the wall that faced the house. He yelled: "Gunlock! Come on out! All that's left is Olaf and one man."

He saw Gunlock coming at a crouching run. Behind him ran Ramón, and behind Ramón, slower, was the cook.

Out at the corral, a man leaped astride a horse, bareback, and spurred away. Up at the house, Irene ran out into the moonlight. Ernie stared at her for a moment with mixed feelings. Part of the blame for all that had happened belonged to Irene. Yet in the end she had done what was right. She had gone to Gunlock with her story; Kirby had told him.

Gunlock passed him, yelling: "Olaf! Don't be a damned fool, man! I don't want you for anything. Ride out if you want."

Olaf's other hired gunman came limping out of the bunkhouse, his hands upraised. Gunlock and Ramón went out of sight behind the bunkhouse. The cook followed, herding the gunman before him. Ernie could hear the sheriff talking, and it could only have been to Olaf that he talked.

Ernie felt his body relax. If Olaf had intended to put up a fight, he'd have done it before now. In a way, it was a relief to Ernie that he didn't. He supposed he should hate Olaf, should want him dead, but somehow the feeling that there had been enough killing tonight was paramount in him. Perhaps that was the reaction from killing Frank.

He holstered his gun and walked toward the house. Irene stared at him, unbelieving. Her face was dead white, but beautiful in the moonlight.

She asked softly, scared still: "Ernie? Is that really you?"

"Yes. It's me." It occurred to him that this was his wife, that this was the wife he had never claimed.

He stared down at her. Her voice was the merest whisper: "Ernie, I'm sorry."

Ernie said, steeling himself against the high fragrance of her: "I killed Frank."

"And Olaf?"

"He's all right. The sheriff is over there talking to him now. I think the sheriff wants to let him go."

"What about you?"

"I'm willing. And as for Dave, I figured all along his heart wasn't in the deal."

He didn't know where to begin this. He didn't even know if he wanted to begin it again. For weeks he had spent his waking hours hating Irene. But standing close to her, it was hard to keep hate alive.

It was she who turned away. She walked back to the house, and Ernie followed. She struck a match and lighted a lamp. For a moment she stood looking at Ernie, her eyes altogether unreadable.

At last she said: "You're thinner. You're pale."

He felt pain replacing the numbness in his shoulder. All of a sudden Irene saw the blood that stained his shirt.

"You're hurt, too. Frank?"

He nodded, and sat down. Gunlock and the cook came in. Gunlock said: "Olaf's leaving. He's taking Frank's body with him. Ramón's helping him get saddled up." Gunlock looked down at Ernie. "Is that all right with you, or do you want to prefer charges?"

Ernie said: "Let him go."

Irene left the room abruptly with a murmured comment about water and bandages. Gunlock waited until she was out of the room. Then he asked: "What about her?"

Ernie didn't answer.

Gunlock said: "If it hadn't been for her, things would've turned out mighty different tonight. You could do a lot worse, boy. Everybody makes mistakes."

Ernie asked: "Where's Matthew?"

"Dead. Kirby killed him. Didn't you know?"

"How the hell could I know?" Ernie blinked. "Kirby?"

Gunlock explained briefly the lawyer's hatred for Matthew.

"And I let Kirby borrow my horse," Ernie said with mild regret, then dismissed it from mind.

He wished he could get his thoughts about Irene straightened out. He wanted her, yet he could not seem to forget that a lot of this had been her fault, that she had been in it with Olaf, cold, calculating, scheming.

She came back into the room, and knelt beside him. She tore his shirt away from his wound. She began to bathe it with a cloth and cold water.

Matthew was dead. It had been hard to believe when Olaf had told him that a month ago. It was harder to believe now. It was hard for Ernie to realize that the iron control that had always governed his life was suddenly gone.

Pain dizzied him as Irene sponged his shoulder. He was thinking of both Olaf and Matthew, comparing them. And suddenly he had the answer. Irene had been no more to blame for this than Ernie himself. Both of them had lived their lives under the iron rule of their fathers. And both of them had done only what they had to do.

He thought about that all the time Irene was bandaging his arm. She stood up, wiping her hands. She said in a still voice: "I'll go pack my things."

Ernie reached up and caught her hand. He pulled her toward him, and used the pull to come out of the chair to his feet. He drew her closely against him. "Do you want to go?"

She hesitated, seeming about to nod. Then she met his eyes. She shook her head, wordless. Ernie smiled, sure and glad, and lowered his lips to hers.

About the Author

Lewis B. Patten wrote more than ninety Western novels in thirty years, and three of them won Spur Awards from the Western Writers of America, and the author received the Golden Saddleman Award. Indeed, this points up the most remarkable aspect of his work: not that there is so much of it, but that so much of it is so fine. Patten was born in Denver, Colorado, and served in the U.S. Navy, 1933–1937. He was educated at the University of Denver during the war years and became an auditor for the Colorado Department of Revenue during the 1940s. It was in this period that he began contributing significantly to Western pulp magazines, fiction that was from the beginning fresh and unique and revealed Patten's lifelong concern with the sociological and psychological affects of group psychology on the frontier. He became a professional writer at the time of his first novel, *Massacre at White River* (1952). The dominant theme in much of his fiction is the notion of justice, and its opposite, injustice. In his first novel it has to do with exploitation of the Ute Indians, but as he matured as a writer he explored this theme with significant and poignant detail in small towns throughout the early West. Crimes, such as rape or lynching, are often at the center of his stories. When the values embodied in these small towns are examined closely, they are found to be wanting. Conformity is always easier than taking a stand. Yet, in Patten's view of the American West, there is usually a man or a woman who refuses to conform. Among his finest titles, always a difficult choice, are surely *Death of a Gunfighter* (1968), *A Death in Indian Wells* (1970), and *The Law at Cottonwood* (1978). No less noteworthy are his previous **Five Star Westerns**, *Tincup in the Storm Country*, *Trail to Vicksburg*, *Death Rides the Denver Stage*, *The Woman at Ox-Yoke*, and *Ride the Red Trail*. His next **Five Star Western** will be *Shadow of the Gun*.